# Run Away to Danger

MAP of THE ... by Abi ...
MARY ROSE

Forecastle

Upper Deck

Main Mast

Castle Deck

Stern Castle

After Castle

Carpenter's Cabin

The Hold

Orlop deck

The Galley

The main Gun Deck

An artist's impression of the *Mary Rose* based on 'Explore the Mary Rose' (by kind permission of the Mary Rose Trust).

# Run Away to Danger

Sandy Norris

For Andrew, Louise and Julie

First published in 2005 by National Maritime Museum Publishing,
Park Row, Greenwich, London, SE10 9NF

*Log on to these websites to play great games and
find out loads more about the Tudors and life at sea:*

www.nmm.ac.uk/tudors

www.nmm.ac.uk/storiesoftheskies

www.nmm.ac.uk/trim

www.portcities.org.uk/london/timepirates

ISBN 0948065605

The characters in this book are fictitious.
Any resemblance to actual persons, living or dead, is purely coincidental.

1 2 3 4 5 6 7 8 9

www.nmm.ac.uk/publishing

Designed and typeset by Carnegie Publishing, Chatsworth Road, Lancaster
Printed and bound in the UK by Alden Press, Oxford

# Author's biography

Born in Malta and brought up on Hayling Island on the South Coast of England, Sandy Norris has always been interested in the sea. Having watched the gradual recovery of the *Mary Rose*, she spent two years, when her children were little, researching the ships of the Tudor Navy and what life would have been like on board, before starting to write her novel. In June 1992, she entered the Portsmouth City Council Creative Writing Competition with the first draft of this story, and won. Currently teaching in Brentwood, Essex, Sandy lives with her family in Maldon on the River Blackwater on the East Coast where her hobbies include swimming and sailing. Having published more than twenty short stories and articles, *Run Away to Danger* is her first full-length work.

# Acknowledgements

I would like to thank my family for their overwhelming support and encouragement, also Andy Elkerton of the Mary Rose Trust, for his expertise and kind support; Eli Dryden at the National Maritime Museum whose dedication has brought this book into being, along with Lyn Stone – illustrator, for visualising my characters and Gill Munton – copy editor, for chasing the logic of the plot through the changes created by three re-writes. I would also like to thank the consultant young readers: Josh Mayne, Bethany Pethers, Megan and Caitlin O'Riordan and Emma Fair and the adult readers: Christine Petrucello and Andrea Cunningham. Lastly, I would like to thank Essex Libraries for enabling me to access many ancient texts for my research.

# Introduction

The *Mary Rose* is the only sixteenth-century warship on display in the world. She was built in 1510, right at the beginning of King Henry VIII's reign and was one of his favourite ships. In 1536 the ship was enlarged and became one of the most modern ships of her time, having been fitted with new-style bronze guns so that she could fire more effectively against the enemy ships.

In July 1545 an enormous French fleet of 200 ships entered the Solent ready to invade the Isle of Wight and to destroy the English fleet. King Henry stood watching from his castle at Southsea while the English fleet hoisted their sails and opened their gun-ports ready to fire against the French, but, to everyone's horror, the *Mary Rose* unexpectedly heeled over and sank. Most of the 500 crewmembers on board drowned as the ship disappeared below the waves and settled into the mud.

In 1971 the *Mary Rose* was rediscovered by Alexander McKee. Hundreds of divers, including HRH Prince Charles, dived repeatedly to excavate the wreck under the water. Finally, in 1982, after more than 400 years on the seabed, *Mary Rose* was gently brought to the surface.

At the Mary Rose Museum today (www.maryrose.org) you can see the hull of the ship for yourself, along with the thousands of items rescued from the seabed: the surgeon's chest and medical equipment, the sailors' bowls, plates and clothes; the musical instruments and board games used to while away the time when they were at sea and many other items, all of which give us a fantastic picture of life on board one of the warships of King Henry VIII.

# Abi

"So what's wrong this time?" Abi snapped, as the heavy cooking pot finished its noisy roll across the stone floor. Her heart turned over as she glanced across the ramshackle room at tiny Mary, who slept undisturbed by the hearth. The pot had missed the baby's head by a hair's breadth. "If you could hold your temper for longer than a day, Ma might not be dead," said Abi, her cheeks flushed and her dark eyes glowering at the hunch-backed man who was her father. Four year-old Davy whimpered and dragged the back of his hand across his nose.

"I never killed your Ma, and you know it," the man wailed, cowering before his daughter's anger. "It weren't my fault she were in the way of the cart. I didn't see her until it were too late." He turned away from her and limped painfully to a stool.

All at once, Abi felt sorry for him, and her expression softened. She knew it had been an accident, but it was six months now since Ma died and none of them had got used to it yet. Pa used to be tall and strong. Now she was taller than he was, although she was only twelve. And he had loved her Ma so much.

But then, as she remembered the pot crashing across the room, her anger returned. "It was you who pushed the cart down the hill." She stood slim and poised like a deer in flight, tensed and ready to move fast if Pa's rage came back.

Davy burst into tears and ran out from under the table to cling to Pa's

1

knees. That settled it. She'd been mulling over the idea for weeks now. If Davy wanted Pa, he could have him. She wasn't going to stay where she wasn't wanted. She swung round and reached for her brown cloak, which was hanging on its nail on the back of the door. She would go and work with her twin brother Tom.

Pa lurched forward and grabbed her arm. "Where are you off to at this time of day?" he growled, his mood turning suspicious.

"Let me go!" shouted Abi, trying to shake him off.

"It's no good you running back to the de Veres." Her father eyed her thoughtfully. "You're no lady's maid. You're only twelve, and it's your place to stay at home and look after the littl'uns. See? It's enough to have that brother of yours always away."

Abi wrenched herself free, pulled the door open and stepped out into the darkening street. She shook her long hair back from her face and ran, breathing deeply so that the cold, clear air worked right into her lungs.

Freedom!

She kept running in case he tried to follow her, her bare feet slapping over the cobbles, the torn hem of her skirt dragging behind her. When she felt a stitch bite into her side, she slowed to a walk. The panic left her then. She knew she was safe; Pa hadn't been able to run since his own accident three years ago when his leg had been crushed under a huge millstone.

Abi crept into Market Square and slipped through the shadows towards the alley which led to the de Veres' house. She mustn't be seen. The night air was chilly, and she pulled her rough cloak more tightly around her shoulders. The last time she'd been here had been

the night Ma died and she was sent for, to go home and look after Davy and Mary. Unbidden, a tear ran down her cheek.

That was the night when "that man" had shouted in his deep voice, threatened Master de Vere, and knocked her down in his furious exit to the stables on the far side of the courtyard. She could still remember the pain in her bruised arm; his powerful fingers had clamped on to it like a ring of steel, trapping her, before he'd hurled her out of the way. She didn't know who the man was, and she hoped to goodness that he wasn't there now.

The back of the house was dim, with only the flicker of candlelight showing in the small panes of the kitchen window. Abi closed the gate quietly, hoping the dogs wouldn't hear, and stood listening. There was a new boy in the kitchen, humming a song. She shivered, and tucked her long skirt between her legs, trying to get warm.

The smell of roasting meat drifted from the house, and Abi's mouth filled with saliva. She hadn't eaten anything since daybreak, and then it had only been a hunk of dry bread and some cheese. The night hardened and folded down around her until her nose hurt with the cold. How long would she have to wait before she could talk to her brother Tom and her cousin Adam? As twins, she and Tom were close, much closer than brother and sister normally were, and she missed him badly. It was just like looking at herself when she looked at him. She grinned instinctively at the thought of his freckled face poking out from under a thorn bush where he'd hidden a few months ago. He must have been desperate to have to do that! His back was covered in tiny scratches from the thorns when he eventually crawled out – but Pa in a bad mood was definitely someone to avoid.

The de Veres' kitchen door opened. Abi listened carefully, and then smiled. It was Seth, the stableboy. Surely he would take a message to Tom and Adam, and help her to find a new place – if not with Mistress de Vere, then perhaps with another family in the town. She had no

intention of stoking the ovens in her Pa's bakery for the rest of her life. She saw Seth pause, his face lit by the rush light he carried, and she called his name softly.

"Who's that?" he whispered.

"It's me, Abigail Penn," she said solemnly, stepping into the ring of light.

"You made me jump," he accused her. Then: "If you're after Adam Tiffany, you're too late."

"Why?"

"He's gone to sea in one of King Henry's ships to work as a surgeon's mate, so you needn't wait around," he smirked.

"You know full well he's my cousin. You must tell me all you know – please, Seth."

"All right," he agreed.

"Fetch Tom!" commanded Abi. Seth paused, and a sudden feeling of dread and emptiness filled Abi's heart.

A voice called out from the kitchen doorway.

"I've got to go," Seth hissed, turning away. "Adam went on the King's ship the *Mary Rose*." Suddenly he pushed hard at her wrist and spun away into the courtyard. "On the River Orwell ... Ipswich ... and your good-for-nothing brother went with him." His voice drifted back, before the door banged and Abi was on her own once more.

Somewhere, away beyond the houses, an owl hooted. A shiver ran right through her and she dropped into a heap on the cold doorstep, more lonely than she'd ever thought possible. So Tom had gone as well.

The sun was disappearing and the day was turning grey. Abi's feet were sore and frozen – she'd run out of the cottage so fast that she'd left her clogs behind. One big toe was bleeding where she'd stubbed it on a rock. She had walked slowly for most of the night, her way lit by the moon. For a couple of hours, she had huddled in a church porch, cross with Tom for leaving her, and wondering if she was right to go on. But when it was dawn, she had forced herself to move, scared of being found. Pa and Davy would have shared her bread between them last night, she thought sourly, as her stomach rumbled with hunger. She felt quite weak.

She guessed her way through the back streets of Ipswich. At least, she hoped this was Ipswich. She didn't want to ask – that would attract too much attention. She felt she must be moving closer to the river; she could hear the mewling of seagulls and she could see these grey-and-white strangers wheeling and plunging above the rooftops.

Abi paused, so tired that her feet no longer wanted to move. The houses were taller here than in Lavenham, and at times she could hardly see the sky. By keeping her eyes on the upper windows she managed to miss the contents of a slop bucket, but she had to hold her nose when a man tipped out his chamber pot. The liquid steamed as it hit the ground. The gutters were choked with rubbish, and the stench of excrement and offal filled her nose so that she wanted to hold her breath. It was unlike anything she'd come across in Lavenham.

She almost gave up. Then, dragging herself forward one last time, she turned a corner and found herself at the waterside. Seamen in short breeches were everywhere, shouting at each other, rolling barrels into line and then loading them into ships' boats. Giant seabirds were everywhere, too, screeching and plunging, fearing no one. A smile pulled Abi's face alive as she walked slowly along the quay. A cold sea breeze blew her hair off her face and cut through her clothing so that she shivered and sneezed, but suddenly, she felt more hopeful.

Then, overwhelmed with so much that was new, she stumbled over a coil of rope that lay to one side of a pile of gentry chests. When she got to her feet she saw a wide river, wider than any she'd ever seen in her life, wide enough for great ships to sail up. She'd never seen so much water. She sniffed. The water stank of the rubbish she could see floating on the surface – the sodden body of a dog thumped repeatedly against the dock as the water swayed and ebbed. But there was something else as well. She sniffed again: salt! How amazing! She hadn't believed Adam when he'd talked about how he planned to go to sea. One day, he'd told her, he'd cross the sea to the Low Countries and set up his own business. He'd take shiploads of wool to sell in the Hague, and bring back Flanders lace to sell to English ladies.

Abi jumped as someone shouted, "Are those chests for the *Mary Rose*?" The reply was lost, but she didn't need to hear it. As far as she could see in the gathering gloom, there were big ships moored out in the water a little way from the dockside. Her heart thumped. One of them must be the *Mary Rose*.

She was still staring at the great ships with their tall masts and tethered sails when a boy went past, and stared at her. That made her think. As she looked down at herself, her heart sank. How could she go on board dressed as what she was: a young girl in her long skirt and apron? Then an idea came to her. As soon as the seamen moved off, she crept up to the last of the chests. Unbelievably, it wasn't locked. The lock looked as if it might be broken. She lifted the lid, climbed in, and dropped down into the darkness.

The strong smell of musk choked her, and a piece of cloth caught against her mouth. She thought she would suffocate and she wanted to scream, but the lid was closed and she was in hiding, waiting to be lifted on board the ship.

After a while, Abi heard a voice. "This is the last one for the *Mary Rose*!" Without warning, she was thrown against one side of the chest, and

only just stopped herself from crying out. Then her whole body was jolted; someone must have dropped the chest into a ship's boat.

The swaying motion of the boat and the mounds of soft cloth in which she lay gradually allowed her to relax. The last voice she heard amongst the squealing and creaking of the boats was deep and strong. It seemed familiar somehow, but in her exhausted state, and shut up in the chest, Abi couldn't think straight. It was a cross voice, shouting orders about something ... Then she slept.

Abi had been dreaming that she was back at work in Mistress de Vere's kitchen. Now she awoke to find herself tangled up in bits of cloth. She pushed at the lid of the chest, but it wouldn't budge. Someone must have tied it shut while she slept. A scream rose inside her, and she clamped her hand tightly over her mouth. Screaming was the last thing she should do.

She turned her attention back to the lid. Perhaps, if she could slip her hand out, she would be able to work it loose. With a lot of grunting and shuffling, she twisted herself into the right position, and then she forced her fingers under the lid. The chest had been tied shut with a leather strap. No matter how hard she tugged and twisted, the leather held firm.

Abi felt her stomach ice over in panic. Then, as the tears began to spill down her face, she realised what she needed. A knife. There must be one somewhere in this chest. Every rich man carried his knives and spoons with him. Trembling, she began to rifle through the layers of shirts and hose and boots.

At last, her fingers closed round a wooden sheath. With difficulty, she removed the knife, slid the blade through the tiny gap, and began to saw her way to freedom.

The leather snapped. Abi pushed the lid back and staggered to her feet, but her legs were painfully cramped. When she slid one leg over the side of the chest and stepped on to the deck, she collapsed and fell. At the same instant, the deck heaved to one side and she rolled across the bare boards, banging painfully into the side of the ship.

For a second, she wondered why she had lost her balance so badly. Then she realised: the ship must be sailing! The *Mary Rose* had left port! What should she do? How would she find Tom and Adam? Sitting up slowly, she tried to look around her. A flickering lantern swayed from a beam above her head. It spiralled round one way, paused, and then began to unwind. It cast strange shadows into the corners, and it was as much as Abi could do to stop herself crying out. She'd never seen the sea before today. Her head hurt where it had crashed into the side of the ship, and tears were rolling down her cheeks. She couldn't stop them. She wondered if she would ever see Davy and tiny Mary again. Although she'd decided to leave home, she hadn't meant to do it this way.

She tried to imagine the sea all around the *Mary Rose*. The water would be rubbing against the boards no more than a few yards away from her. The air smelled damp and unfriendly, and she shivered. There must be some boy's garments somewhere among all these boxes and chests. Once she'd changed her clothes, she would stand less chance of being discovered.

Eventually, by crawling across the tilting deck, she managed to reach the smaller chests near the back of the pile. She had to be careful; she'd noticed some of the seamen asleep in the far corner. The last thing she wanted was to wake them, although with luck, the constant groaning of the ship's timbers would hide any sounds she made. At the second attempt she found what she was looking for. She tore off her skirt and apron, and pulled on a pair of dark woollen hose and some brown breeches. She was shivering violently by the time she had

laced herself into the leather jerkin, and it wasn't just because she was cold. If anyone had woken up and seen her ... She couldn't imagine what would have happened. Lastly, she pulled out a brown knitted cap and wound her long hair into it.

In the dim light she picked her way over to a ladder leading to the deck above. She was beginning to feel horribly sick. The ship rolled again as she climbed, and she shut her eyes and prayed, her fingernails digging into the rough wood of the handrail. She still couldn't think straight. The constant screeching of the ship's timbers was enough to drive anyone mad. Never in all her twelve years had she come across anything like it. With the ship stable for a few seconds, she scurried across the deck to another ladder, and started climbing again. As she climbed, she gave a fleeting thought to the rows of sleeping bodies in the shadows.

Suddenly, a breeze was blowing in her face, and the strong, salty air made her sneeze again. She had reached the open deck. Breathing deeply with relief, she looked around her.

It was almost night. There was a tiny light on a half-deck behind her, a second directly above that, and a third, merely a pinprick, right at the back. All around her, she could hear the powerful sea sluicing against the ship's sides.

Suddenly, she heard a scuffle overhead and a deep, angry voice. Her heart missed a beat. Two men were leaning against a rail on the half-deck, their feet on a level with her head. She crept off to hide behind a huge gun which was battened up against the ship's side. In a strange way, it made her think of home and Hedingham Castle which was only a day's walk away – she had seen those guns several times.

She poked her head cautiously round the breech end of the gun, and saw the taller man shake his fist. Something was definitely not right here. Then he thumped the handrail, but with the howling of the wind and the swish of the waves, she could not hear what he said. Then the

men were struggling with each other. Round and round they tumbled, first one and then the other being forced against the handrail. As the men rolled over and over, she caught glimpses of their angry faces and their raised fists. It was like the play in the Market Square that she'd gone to see with Tom, when St George had fought with the dragon. But that had been a man pretending, and this was real.

Abi left her hiding place and crept up a ladder which connected the two decks. She lifted her head over the rim of the half-deck just in time to see one of the men fall. She imagined rather than heard the thump of his head crashing on to the hard wood. Then the other man was on top of him, punching at his chest and face as he writhed and struggled like a wild animal. They rolled over, and she caught a flash of colour as they crashed into the big mast under the lantern. The one on top was wearing knee-length red leather boots. Then they moved back into the gloom.

Abi climbed down again, her heart thumping. Her body wouldn't stop shuddering and her teeth rattled together like bones. She'd seen enough. If she was careful, she might be able to creep below without the men noticing. But the instant she reached the lower deck, she heard a muffled shout. It was followed seconds later by a splash. She ran to look over the side of the ship, and saw a dark shape rising above the water and drifting against the timbers.

She tried to scream, but no sound came out; she was too shaken. Then, glancing up, she saw the man with the red boots looking over the side of the ship, watching the body's progress. It must be a body, she felt certain. She shuddered again, this time from fear. How could this have happened to her? First, the *Mary Rose* had sailed with Abi on board, and now she'd witnessed what looked like a murder!

Looking neither left nor right, Abi tumbled down ladder after ladder and ran across deck after deck, until she could go no further. She stopped, and peered about her. This must be the very bottom of the

ship, the hold. Dimly, she could see the base of the main mast. Piles of birch logs and other bulky stores stood against the sides of the ship. The stench was overpowering – a damp, closed-in smell that made her feel trapped, and sent a stone of clammy fear into the pit of her stomach.

She walked a few paces, her feet crushing the shingle ballast. But then she tripped and fell, bruising her shins as she knocked against something cold and hard. For an instant, she pictured her father as he'd stood when she last saw him, and wondered why she'd been so foolish as to leave home. With Tom already gone, who would pick Davy up when he fell over? Who would cuddle tiny Mary?

On hands and knees, Abi crawled towards the main mast. With her back to its base, she braced herself against the continual rolling of the ship. Her mind kept seeing the men's raised fists as they rolled in and out of the light of the pitching lantern nailed to the mast.

When Abi woke up, she had no idea whether it was night or day. Down in the hold, the darkness was unchanging. She shivered, and drew her knees up against her chest. Her stomach rumbled with hunger, and the back of her throat felt dry. She ought to try to find the boys. Adam, at least, would know what to do about the two men, as well as how to cope with her own plight. He was a sensible boy, Ma had always said.

It took her a while to realise that the darkness had grown darker, and the sounds were more muffled. Someone had closed the hatch leading up to the next deck! She was trapped! In panic, she stumbled towards the base of the ladder and hauled herself up, feeling her way blindly.

The ladder seemed to go on for ever. For a moment, Abi thought she was climbing up the thatching ladder that had been propped against the wall of their cottage last summer. If anything, the ship's motion

had become more violent. Her head banged hard against the hatch. She jerked backwards, almost pitching off the ladder and into the dark hole below. Her heart thumping, she raised her hands to the hatch. She pushed, but nothing moved. Then she pushed harder, banging against the wood. Still nothing.

The *Mary Rose* was like an enormous animal with a rolling gait, and she was trapped in its belly, unable to escape. For a long time, she forced herself to sit still, her back against the mast. If she stayed there, at least she knew where she was. If she moved about in the nightmarish darkness of the hold, she wouldn't know what was real and what was make-believe. The noise of the water thundering against the side of the ship was deafening. And all she could think of was the fight, and then looking over the side and seeing the body ...

After a while, Abi sensed that someone was watching her. She told herself not to be silly. Carefully, she scanned the dark spaces around her. Nothing. Of course not! But then suddenly, she felt rather than heard a movement a little way off, somewhere between her body and the bottom of the ladder. Then she saw it – an enormous rat! It rose up on its hind legs, twitching its whiskers as it cleaned itself. She could imagine that it was sniffing at her body.

She gulped, and bit back a scream. She pushed herself hard against the mast, but all she could really do was to stay as still as possible. She knew what rats were like. It would all depend on when this one had last eaten. Unbidden, her mind brought forth an image of last spring in Lavenham, when she had come across a big black rat in a child's cot – busy gnawing away at the child's face ... No doubt the mother was simply trying to give her baby some clean air after the long winter.

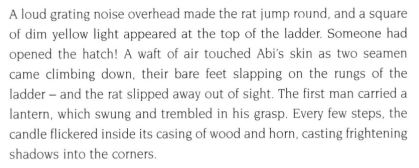

A loud grating noise overhead made the rat jump round, and a square of dim yellow light appeared at the top of the ladder. Someone had opened the hatch! A waft of air touched Abi's skin as two seamen came climbing down, their bare feet slapping on the rungs of the ladder – and the rat slipped away out of sight. The first man carried a lantern, which swung and trembled in his grasp. Every few steps, the candle flickered inside its casing of wood and horn, casting frightening shadows into the corners.

Abi scrambled to her feet, her heart still thumping. She edged round the mast, out of sight of the ladder, and clung to its rope wolding, hoping that the sounds of the ship would hide the crunch of her footsteps in the ballast. When the men climbed up again, she'd have to find some way of following them before they closed the hatch. Her chest felt tight, and she thought she would burst if she had to stay down in this pit for much longer.

For a while, the men were shifting barrels in the stern. Then the ship heaved, and seemed to turn completely on to its side, its timbers groaning in the force of the waves. One of the men shrieked as a pile of logs slipped and crashed down on top of him. His continuous howls made Abi wince at the thought of the pain. They reminded her of Pa's accident with the millstone. She crept closer, staying in the shadows. The man's left leg was pinned down by a huge log.

More men, wearing wide, loose breeches, climbed down the ladder. With much muttering, the seamen set to work to clear the wood from the man's leg. His howls turned into groans. Abi longed to go and support his head and soothe him, but she didn't dare.

As they pulled the man free, another arrived. Abi stared at him curiously, because he looked so different from the others. He was dressed in black, and he appeared to be a lot older. He brought with him a distinct smell – of herbs, and something sickly-sweet that Abi

didn't recognise. One of the seamen helped him down the ladder, saying, "He's down here, Surgeon."

Abi's heart leaped at the word. Seth had said that Adam was to help the Surgeon. Well, here he was. All she had to do now was to follow the crowd when they went back up the ladder, and with luck she might find Adam and Tom.

After what seemed a long time, the men in the rescue party tied the injured man on to a makeshift stretcher and fixed ropes to one end. Two of them climbed through the hatch and started to pull, with the others guiding the stretcher upwards. The man, with his poor, crushed leg, was writhing in agony. The smell of his blood was even stronger than the stagnant damp stench of the hold.

Cautiously, Abi crept along at the back of the party. Perhaps no one would notice her in the half-light – her long hair was still tucked up in her boy's cap. Her heart pounded as she clambered up the ladder after the last man. Then she stepped on to the lantern-lit deck.

On both sides, Abi glimpsed the back ends of enormous guns facing heavy, closed shutters. In a battle, she guessed, they would be pushed through the shutters and made ready to fire. Now they were tethered, to stop them moving.

All around the deck, caught in the glimmer of the lanterns as they twisted and turned in the swaying motion of the ship, were men and boys. Some were curled up alongside their guns, sound asleep. Others were whittling away at linstocks. There was a subdued mutter of conversation, and as Abi staggered and fought to keep her balance, she strained to hear what they were talking about. But the ship constantly shifted and groaned, drowning out all other sounds.

The seamen carrying the stretcher moved quite naturally, without any effort, but Abi's legs found muscles she didn't know she had. Just as she was wondering what to do next, the familiar figure of Adam appeared in a doorway. Adam, tall and slim, with his scruff of fair hair

that always looked untidy. At last! She wanted to rush forward and let him know she was there, but instead, she made herself shuffle along at the back of the little procession.

When the patient was in the Surgeon's cabin, Abi went up to her cousin and tugged at his sleeve. He looked round, faintly irritated. Then his eyes widened in amazement, and Abi put a finger to her lips. After a long pause, Adam smiled and nodded. He turned his back and went to the Surgeon's aid.

Abi followed her cousin through the narrow doorway into the tiny cabin. Immediately, she was overwhelmed by the sickly smell she'd noticed around the Surgeon when they were in the hold. It must be the smell of his herbs and potions.

Half the space in the cabin was taken up by a rough wooden bench, and it was here that the injured man was laid. A lantern hung from a central beam.

"Out, all of you!" shrilled the Surgeon, his black bonnet bobbing with his words. "How can I do my work with a cabin full of sailors?" The seamen backed out, leaving Abi and Adam with the Surgeon and the injured man. The Surgeon stared at Abi and opened his mouth to speak, but at that moment, the man on the bench grunted.

Instantly, the Surgeon turned back to attend to him. "Hold him down, will you?" He indicated the man's good leg and his arms. Adam stepped forward, but Abi hung back, uncertain. "What are you waiting for, boy?" snapped the Surgeon, grabbing her arm and yanking her forward. "You ought to know what to do by now."

She knew that Adam must be grinning because the Surgeon had mistaken her for Tom. But she still didn't know what to do. The injured man lay unresisting, but his eyes darted around the room. His hair was wet with sweat, and his body stank where he'd messed himself in his terror.

"Hold hard!" shouted the Surgeon, as he attacked the wound with a delicate vigour that made Abi gasp. With cloths soaked in alcohol, he sponged out the long gash, filling cloth after cloth with blood. The patient struggled as he tried to move away from the pain; he was almost too strong for Abi and Adam to hold down.

The Surgeon uncorked two tiny ceramic jars. He tipped liquids on to a sponge, and clamped it over the man's nose and mouth. "Opium and hemlock," Adam muttered in Abi's ear. "They will calm him, and help with the pain."

Gradually, the patient's struggling lessened, though Abi was still aware of his scared eyes staring up at her. She couldn't stop trembling; she was fascinated and excited, sick and terrified all at the same time. The Surgeon took a long needle and some thread. He nipped the sides of the gash together and stitched through the flesh. Sick flooded into Abi's mouth, and she caught sight of Adam's sympathetic gaze as she turned to retch on to the floor. She sighed and grinned; my first act as a boy! Not exactly convincing. Then she looked back at the patient and the long line of stitches sinking into his flesh, intrigued by the Surgeon's skill.

At last all was done, and the man was carried away to sleep. Watching the Surgeon's back view as he scrubbed his hands clean of blood, Abi wondered when the questions would come. She didn't have to wait long.

"Well, boy." The man in black turned to look at her in a kindly but determined way. The sleeve of his robe caught in the pot of alcohol. "Drat", he said, and flung it out of the way. "You've been on this ship a good few weeks now, yet you failed to help me when I needed you to!" He paused and looked straight at her, a half-puzzled smile on his face. "You look the same and yet different, and I haven't seen you in those clothes before. What's going on?"

Abi looked at her feet. She didn't know what to say. She could feel the

Surgeon's stare fixed on her as he waited. High above her head, on another deck, she heard a man's voice calling. Seconds later, she heard the pounding of feet on wood as the crew rushed to change the sails and the ship started to lean as it turned. Abi was hungry and exhausted and her mind was blank.

# Tom

Tom halted abruptly in the doorway of the Surgeon's cabin. Was it a ghost? It couldn't be his sister Abi – she was at home in Lavenham! Was she trying to tell him he shouldn't have left her? Tom shivered.

He'd just slipped up to the weather deck to watch the younkers work the sails. By crouching under the boat amidships, he could cling on to the bottom of it unseen and watch the men working the ship. The wind was beginning to blow quite strongly and spray had lashed his face, yet he had loved every minute of it. Life at sea was so open and free. So different from life in Lavenham. The *Mary Rose* was constantly on the move, and there was so much that was new and exciting. He still couldn't believe that Adam had asked him to come with him. He, Tom, was only twelve – but if Adam was learning about life on board, that was what he wanted to do, too.

But he'd felt guilty about leaving his work. He'd made his way back to the Surgeon's cabin to find out whether he'd been missed and, if so, what his punishment might be.

And here he was, not believing his eyes as he looked at his sister. What was she doing on board the *Mary Rose*? He'd last seen her two months ago in their tiny cottage, pulling a face at Pa as he, Tom, hovered on the doorstep, anxious to be gone. He'd felt sorry for her, but she was the girl. Somebody had to stay and look after the younger children. He studied the familiar yet unfamiliar figure, with the tip-tilted nose and freckles just like his own. She was dressed as a boy and he couldn't think where she'd found all the clothes, but in her brown

19

leather jerkin and with her knitted cap hiding her hair, she looked uncannily like himself.

Adam winked at Tom, and he pulled himself together. He stepped into the small space and said, "I think my brother is looking for work, Surgeon."

Abi risked a glance upwards. The Surgeon gaped, his head turning from one twin to the other.

"Twins! Why didn't you say?" He smiled, and Tom let out a slow breath. Without even realising it, he had stopped breathing the moment he had seen Abi.

"I didn't realise it was Kit to start with," Adam was saying. "He's changed a lot since I last saw him." He grinned at Abi.

Tom felt better now. He knew Adam would get it right. Thank goodness he'd kept his wits about him.

At last, Abi found her tongue. "I do need work, Surgeon, if you'll have me." She tilted her head to one side and looked up into the man's eyes. Then she turned and smiled her cheeky, dimpled smile at Tom.

He found himself clenching his hands so tightly that his nails were digging into the palms of his hands. He smiled back wryly at his sister. She was always faster than he was, and she'd known he was there even before she looked up. She had to make the Surgeon believe her, or they would be in real trouble.

"Our Ma's dead, and Pa's too busy in his bakery to want me around." Tom saw Abi cross her fingers as she spoke, and he automatically crossed his own. "He's got himself a new wife to look after the littl'uns, so he doesn't need me any more. He kicked me out of the house yesterday, told me to make my own way in the world." She spread her hands wide. "So here I am. I've come to join my brother."

Tom turned spontaneously to his twin, and raised a clenched fist – their private signal that things were going well. But they still faced a nasty

situation. Girls – and women – weren't allowed on board any ship. It was said to be bad luck! He knew that much. Then his mind filled with horror as he thought about what might happen if they were found out – Abi put off the ship at the first port, and, most probably, himself and Adam locked in the hold as a punishment. He forced himself to smile.

"Hmm . . ." The Surgeon's left eyebrow twitched. "We'd better take you to the Captain's Steward. He has to know who's on board," he muttered, more to himself than to the three "lads". Abi glanced at Adam in alarm.

"But didn't you say you could do with an extra mate?" he asked quickly.

The Surgeon lifted his chin to stare at the older boy. "I did, but . . . aha, I see what you mean!" he said, a slow smile spreading across his face. "You mean that if we don't announce young . . ."

"Kit."

"Young Kit's appearance, we'll find it easier to keep a hold on him." The Surgeon stopped, thought, and then nodded his head. "So be it." Then he turned back to his medicine chest. "You'd better show him what his duties will be, if he's not to stand out like a sore thumb."

Tom breathed a sigh of relief.

Adam smiled. "Thank you, Master. Come on, young Kit." He turned his face away from the Surgeon, and winked at Abi. "You're very lucky," he said, trying but failing to look serious. Then he bent down and whispered into her ear. "We'll have to fix you up with a haircut, coz!"

# Abi

Later, Abi was sitting next to Tom and Adam on the orlop deck. She had planned to have a row with her twin when she caught up with him. How could he have abandoned her and gone away to sea? But just surviving the last few hours had made that question seem unimportant.

21

She felt worn out. The Surgeon had kept them busy all forenoon, helping to look after injured seamen. Every half-hour, when the sails needed readjusting because of the storm, someone was injured. One man had fallen down the main hatch and landed on his head ...

She leaned back against the wooden boarding above the galley, seeking some comfort from the lingering warmth of the cook's forenoon fire. It had been doused in case it set the ship alight; it would only need a few shooting sparks to catch the wood.

Up on deck the wind still raged, the force of the waves tipping the ship from side to side. Abi cupped her hands round the tankard of ale that Adam had scrounged for her, sipping it slowly to make it last, and let her head nod drowsily.

But just as she was slipping into a dream, she heard the buzz of sailors' voices. She listened carefully, pretending to be asleep.

A rumour was growing. Where was Edward Ferris, the Captain's Lieutenant of the Militia? No one had seen him today. Had he fallen overboard? A skinny lookout boy called Henty said he'd heard Ferris arguing with someone as he'd climbed down the mast from the last dogwatch, but no one knew who it was.

Abi's stomach sank as she put two and two together. The body she'd watched as it bobbed against the side of the ship last night – it must have been Edward Ferris! And the murderer (she felt no doubt that it *was* murder) was someone on the ship ...

She ought to do something, tell someone. But who, and how? She wasn't even supposed to be on the ship, and she didn't have any proof that it was murder. She just knew.

She thought back. The only detail she remembered was the quick flash of red boots as the two men rolled into the mast where the lantern hung. And then she had seen the man with red boots looking over the rail. That was all.

This was a matter for Adam. He was sixteen. He would know what to do.

"Adam, I need to tell you something." She could hear the panic in her voice, and tried to speak more calmly.

"What the . . .?" Adam roused himself from his doze.

"Adam! Please come back to the Surgeon's cabin!" she whispered, willing him to understand. "I need your help." She tugged at his sleeve. "It's important!"

"It had better be, young coz," moaned Adam. He pulled himself to his feet, followed by Tom.

Abi turned and moved forward, stumbling over someone's legs in the half-dark. Adam walked slowly and reluctantly, and Abi had to drop back to speak to him, prancing like a restless foal. "I saw it!" she declared. "I've got to tell someone, and you're the only one who'll understand." She led the way up the ladder, along the deck and into the Surgeon's cabin. Luckily, there was no one there.

"What d'you mean?" asked Adam, still sleepy from his nap. "You saw what?"

"The murder! Everyone's wondering where Master Ferris is. I think he was murdered – and I saw it happen! I was up on deck when the two men were fighting . . ."

"Murder?" hissed Tom in disbelief.

Suddenly wide awake, Adam poked his head out through the doorway to check that no one was within hearing distance. "Here – start rolling these up," he said, thrusting a mound of bandages into Abi's arms. "Now, tell me what happened."

"I hid in a chest to come on board the *Mary Rose*. Later, I managed to get out of the chest, and I went up on deck . . ."

"Was it light? Could you see?" interrupted Adam.

Tom merely nodded in sympathy. He would know exactly what she meant. He nearly always did.

"No – it was dark, and I didn't know where I was, or which deck was which. I hid behind one of the big guns ..." She told them the rest of the story.

"Keep rolling." Adam nodded at her hands. "We need to look busy."

Abi jumped as the cabin door suddenly squeaked open. A head appeared.

"Captain's Steward, Master Henry Pole," Adam muttered as he stood to attention. "Here we go."

"Where is Surgeon Spencer?" growled the Steward, flicking a piece of dirt from the shoulder of his immaculate leaf-green doublet. "You, boy! Find him for me!" He cuffed Adam across the head. "And be quick about it, or I'll have you flogged. I have a stomach ague, and I need a comfort." With that, he turned and disappeared into the gloom of the main deck. Adam slipped out after him on his errand while the twins turned back to their bandages.

Abi's heart missed a beat. That was the cross voice she'd heard on the quay when she was hidden in the chest – and this, unbelievably, was the man who had knocked into her at the de Veres' house on the night when their Ma had died! She glanced at her brother, and then realised that he wouldn't react; he hadn't been there when it had happened. She shivered. What did it all mean?

She heard the Surgeon calling her, and hurriedly dumped her pile of bandages. She rushed to the doorway, forgetting the motion of the boat, and had to cling to the doorpost to stop herself sprawling on the deck.

"Take Master Pole a dose of rose water, Kit." Impatiently, the Surgeon grabbed a small brown jar and held it out to Abi.

She felt faint. Then she smiled to herself. There was no need to be

nervous – she didn't look at all like the girl Pole had knocked out of the way in Lavenham.

The deck creaked like a living creature. To a girl used to the quiet of the countryside, the constant sounds and movements were unnerving. Reluctantly, she made her way to Henry Pole's cabin as she'd been directed. She knocked on the door, and struggled to open it when she heard his arrogant voice: "Enter!"

But the door had jammed, and wouldn't shift. Frustrated, Abi tried again, bruising her fingers. Then the Steward forced the door open from the other side, making Abi lose her balance and stumble through the doorway. She landed in an undignified heap at Master Pole's feet, with her face almost touching his tall brown boots.

"Get up, boy!" the man said contemptuously. "Why are you so clumsy?"

"I'm sorry," stuttered Abi. Why hadn't the Surgeon sent Tom? It wasn't fair! But perhaps he was testing her. She staggered along the boards again as she tried to keep hold of the jar of rose water and stand up at the same time. But at the crucial second, a wave crashed against the side of the ship, knocking her back down.

"Could you hold this for me while I get up, please?" she asked, offering the rose water to the Steward, who towered above her.

"I? Hold that for *you*?" He laughed nastily. Then he swung his fist and aimed it at Abi's head. Sheer terror helped her to her feet as she ducked to avoid the blow. She handed him the jar. Turning away with a muttered "Sorry", she stumbled through the narrow doorway. Fighting against the tilt of the deck, she found her way back to the Surgeon's cabin, her heart thudding in her chest.

Later, once the night watch was in place, the wind eased a little and the deck seemed less like a wild animal. Abi, Tom and Adam were crammed into Adam's hammock at one end of the orlop deck, with a long piece of sacking wrapped round them. They huddled together, for warmth – and for secrecy.

"Henry Pole, at the de Veres'. I know when you mean," Adam said slowly, chewing over the thought. He fiddled with a rope as the hammock swung in time to the movement of the ship. "He's been to see Master de Vere several times, although his family are only yeomen. The de Veres seem to look after him. I guess they got him his commission on this ship."

"What's he got to do with what we're supposed to be talking about?" Tom burst out in frustration, his eyes flashing. He pointed at his twin. "And what about Abi?" he hissed. "She's not supposed to be here, remember – she's a girl! How can we do anything about anything without getting into trouble?"

"Shh. Don't tell the whole ship." Adam turned to Abi. "You mentioned red boots. Was there nothing else?"

"No."

## Tom

Tom looked from one to the other. He was confused. It was all far too vague, he thought. It seemed to him that Abi and Adam were drifting off the point. He liked to know what was what straight away. He hated mysteries. He eyed his sister, but realised instantly that she was shut away from him. In the half-dark he could see little, but from years of practice, he could sense that she was deep in thought.

"The way he hit out at Adam this forenoon," she muttered.

Tom put on his sarcastic, irritated voice. "Who are you talking about now?" He knew he shouldn't speak to his sister like that – his Ma

would have told him off – but he couldn't help it. She shouldn't keep secrets from him.

"Master Pole."

"What's he got to do with ..." he threw back, but Adam was quicker.

"You mean, you think that the murderer, the man in Lavenham and Henry Pole might all be the same person?" he said in a voice so low that the twins could hardly hear him.

Abi turned, and Tom could see her eyes shining in excitement. "Yes, that's exactly what I mean."

"Shh – not so loud!" Tom glanced round, worried, but no one was taking any notice of a hammock full of boys.

The three paused for thought. Around them the deck continued to squeak and groan, the sea foaming and churning against the outer skin of the ship. On all sides, life on board continued in much the same way as it always did at night. Mounds of sleeping bodies had flopped down on the hard deck. A few groups of men could be seen with a lantern slung from a nail, moving pieces across a board or playing backgammon. At the far end, Tom glimpsed the tiny body of Henty, clutching his pipe as he slept.

"We need evidence," Adam said very seriously. "You'll have to get into Henry Pole's cabin, Abi, and make sure that he does have a pair of red boots. He certainly wasn't wearing them today. Then we'll work out what to do after that."

Tom swayed as he stood on the quarterdeck, pulling his woollen hat more firmly down over his ears. The breeze was strong; the grey November sky was filled with scudding, off-white clouds, and there was a fresh, salty tang in the air.

Until Abi arrived, life on board had been one big adventure – even if he didn't really like working for the Surgeon. He'd always wanted to go to sea, and he couldn't believe his luck when Adam suggested that they go together. Sailing on the *Mary Rose*, one of King Henry's biggest ships, was amazing; he'd never expected anything so exciting to happen to him. After all, the Penns were not well off – not like Adam's family. The Tiffanys had worked for the de Veres for half a lifetime, and were almost treated as part of the family.

But now, here was Abi with all these questions. Typical of a girl, he thought – even if the girl was Abi.

He reached for a handhold as the deck tilted more steeply. Excitement had fast changed to anxiety with his sister's appearance, and the thought of what might happen to them when she was found to be a girl. Tom shivered, thinking back a few hours. Piers Jolland, the Steward's assistant, had been unkind to Abi ever since he'd met the twins. He was never pleasant, but Abi really seemed to get on his nerves. He just kept on picking on her, no matter what she did.

To larboard, quite a long way off on the horizon, Tom could see the *Peter* and the *Minion*. They were supposedly on a parallel tack to the *Mary Rose*, although he found it difficult to tell. The *Murrayann* lay further east. He knew that – the ship's Master had told him. The others were strung out, too far away to recognise.

The wind blew ever more strongly, clearing away the last shreds of sleep. Tom realised that he was ravenous. He could imagine biting into a thick hunk of cheese with a slice of beef, and he could easily down a tankard of ale – but that would have to wait until the Captain had eaten.

A tap on his shoulder told him that Abi had arrived. He smiled, but as soon as she had crept into the shelter beside him, Piers stuck his head out of the main hatch.

"So that's where you are! No more skulking for you two – the Captain's breakfast is needed, and his cabin has to be swept out first. Come

along!" he snarled. He caught hold of Abi's ear and dragged her after him. It didn't seem to matter that the Surgeon wanted the twins to work with him, Tom thought wryly; Piers just ignored the older man's wishes, and ordered them to do his bidding.

"Stop that, you brute. You don't know ..." Horrified, Tom let his words fall away.

"What did you say?" Piers loosened his hold on Abi, his face hard and disdainful. "What don't I know?" He stood firm, his body angling to the deck as the ship tilted. "What's so special about your brother? Don't tell me we have a prince in disguise," he sneered, his lip curling in disdain.

"Piers, please." Abi touched his arm. "He didn't mean to be rude. It's just that he was born first, and he always thinks that he should protect ..." She trailed off as Piers stared at her.

"Weakling!" he spat. "Trust me to get landed with a puny weakling for a servant!" Then he started towards the ladder to the upper deck, the twins following reluctantly.

It occurred to Tom that he could say that they weren't Piers' servants, that the Surgeon wanted them to work for him – but it didn't seem like the best idea in the world to argue with Master Jolland.

Tom sighed deeply. His head was full of the whining of the wind in the rigging, the slap and bang of the sails and the wonderful way the ship buffeted along through the churning sea. If only Abi were safe in Lavenham, feeding baby Mary, he wouldn't need to worry about her.

Piers strode through an archway towards the Captain's cabin at the stern of the ship, and the twins ran after him. "One of you had better go to the galley and bring up the Captain's breakfast," he snapped. He pushed his way through a sliding door and into the cabin. "Bring a manchet loaf and the best cheese – and bring some slices of gammon."

Tom turned back, reluctant to leave "Kit" in Piers' company, and yet glad to have something to do. He shrugged, and groped his way back to the comparative dark of the gun deck.

A gale, the Master had said. And a gale it was beginning to feel like as he began to struggle through the pitching ship. The *Mary Rose* lurched uncomfortably in the shifting sea, and Tom's stomach squirmed and tumbled. The weather was worsening rapidly.

# Abi

When Tom left her to fetch the Captain's breakfast, Abi felt a wave of dislike sweep through her. She only just resisted the urge to hurry after her brother. Instead she waited, outwardly steady but with a queasy stomach, to see what Piers would say next. She was so close to the spineless bully that she could smell the musk on his neck.

Together, Abi and Piers opened one of the chests, folded the soft bedding from the Captain's bed, and dropped it in. How nice to be a captain, she thought, fingering the smooth wool. Not for the likes of her.

She picked up the lantern that had stood to one side of the bed, and tried to hang it on a hook above her head. She couldn't reach, and Piers snatched the lantern impatiently. He reached up and lit the candle. Abi turned back and started to walk back to the chest, but at that moment the ship heeled sharply to starboard. In her efforts to regain her balance, she reached for the door. But before she had it in her grasp, the ship slewed back to port and she was sent careering into the solid body of Piers.

He grabbed her arm roughly. "What d'you think you're doing, land boy? Should you even be at sea? You look too much of a mother's boy to me." He gripped both her arms tightly, shaking her so that her head jerked backwards and forwards. Abi closed her eyes, crossing her

fingers and willing her cap to stay on. Adam had hacked away her long hair, but without the cap on, Tom had told her that she still looked like a girl.

"Why don't you leave him alone, Piers?" said a calm voice from the corner. "He won't be any good to you as a servant if you shake him up too much; he'll spend all his time being sick." The voice sounded friendly, and Abi risked opening her eyes. She saw a boy with wide-set grey eyes and a smiling face. He was about the same height as Piers and about Adam's age – though without Adam's muscles. He had slightly stooping shoulders inside a black doublet. The boy looked at her intently. Piers grunted and released his grip.

For a moment, only the groaning of the timbers and the howling wind could be heard. A wave washed across the glass porthole, and the corkscrewing lantern on the deck head cast strange distorted shadows on the boys' faces. The sky had become quite dark. Abi straightened herself, pulled her cap back into position, and opened her mouth to speak – but one look at Piers' grim features made her clamp it shut again.

The door slid open and Tom appeared, carrying a tray of food. Piers moved to snatch it away from him. "Just you wait!" he growled. He set the tray down, and barged past Tom to the door. "I have to call ... Captain Grenville!" He paused on the name, as if to emphasise how important a servant he was. "Fetch the Captain's platters and knives from the chest, and a bowl for his prunes. I hope you brought some prunes," he aimed at Tom. "And make sure you're not here when I return."

"Charming, isn't he?" said the older boy, reaching into the chest for the pewter platters and bowls. "I'm Martin Talbot, the Captain's Clerk – but most of the time I feel like one of Piers' lackeys, the same as you," he grinned, pushing his hair back out of his eyes. "Now, what he didn't tell you is that you need to fold away the Captain's bed as well as the

bedding, and to sweep the floor. He's hoping that if he brings the Captain back into a messy room, he'll have an excuse to beat you."

The three of them tugged the unwieldy mattress off the bed and tipped it untidily into a long wooden chest.

"It's best to keep out of his way as much as possible." Martin grimaced, and then grinned. "Not that there's much room on board for hiding." He looked hard at Abi, and then at Tom. "You're twins, aren't you? But one of you has been around a lot longer. I've seen you with the Surgeon. Why didn't you come on board together?"

"I was supposed to stay and look after my Pa and the younger children after our Ma died. I'm the younger twin, so Tom was allowed to come to sea with our cousin Adam, and I had to stay at home. But then I got so mad with Pa that I ran away." Abi crossed her fingers. She didn't like telling lies, but it wasn't far from the truth. "And so I walked to Ipswich, and found the *Mary Rose*."

The door squeaked open again, and Piers reappeared. He caught sight of the twins, and leaped at Abi, cuffing her over the head. "I thought I told you to get out! Now, when I say get out, I mean get out, you ignorant child – and you as well!" He prodded Tom in the back.

Abi lost her temper. With a flounce, she turned to Piers. "Don't you call me ignorant!" she shrieked furiously, seeing but ignoring Tom's horrified expression out of the corner of her eye. "I'm not ignorant. I know more than you do. Those red boots, for instance. I ..."

Fortunately, Captain Grenville appeared in the doorway at that moment. Abi was already regretting her words, and hating the way Tom was looking at her. "We'd better go," she muttered, not daring to catch Martin's eye. While Piers was busy fussing around, she scurried out of the cabin, followed by Tom – although not before Captain Grenville had given them a long stare. As they hurried to the ladder that would take them down to the open gun deck, Abi distinctly heard Piers telling the Captain that having twins as servants had given him

"two for the price of one!" What a cheek, she thought, but she wasn't about to protest.

# Tom

As Tom hurried after his sister across the tilting deck, he heard urgent voices. Several seamen were leaning over the side of the ship, shouting to each other as they tried to cut through a great tangle of ropes. Tom looked back over his shoulder as he ran – and in the space of a few seconds, Abi disappeared from view.

He groped his way through the clumps of men who crouched in every available space. The air was so thick he could hardly breathe. He felt damp and sweaty, but cold at the same time. The deck was running with water from the rough sea, yet a couple of seamen were managing to sleep amidst all the chaos.

Tom dropped down to the orlop deck, and finally caught up with his sister. "Sorry!" she muttered. Together, they scrambled along to the galley, where they pressed their hands against the bulkhead to warm them.

Tom sighed. For the moment, he refused to consider what problems might have been set in motion by Abi's slip about the red boots. No doubt Piers would hound them when he was ready.

# Abi

Two days after Abi's outburst, they sailed into Portsmouth Harbour. The anchor dropped with a splash, and the *Mary Rose* swung on her chain. The sails seemed to have disappeared, furled against their spars as if by magic.

There had been two days of frenzied activity to repair the storm damage to the ship – and two days of Abi dodging out of sight the minute she heard Piers' voice. Fortunately, Surgeon Spencer had given

her plenty of work; a large number of men had been hurt during the gale. After that first sighting of an open wound, she had found that she wasn't squeamish, and the Surgeon had started to rely on her as his best assistant – after Adam, of course.

But her nerves were constantly on edge. Only yesterday forenoon, Piers had appeared in the doorway of the Surgeon's cabin, and grabbed her round the neck. She shouted and his hand shot over her mouth, so that she tasted the salty grime of unwashed skin. "What didn't you want to tell me?" he hissed. "What were you going to say about red boots?" He twisted her arm behind her back and jerked it up, sending shooting pains into her shoulder and making her gasp.

Then Abi heard the Surgeon's voice outside the cabin, and it was Piers' turn to gasp. In a single movement, he released her arm, threw her to the deck and shot out through the doorway. She flopped down, grazing her head on the uneven surface. She was bruised, but defiant.

"What's the matter, young Kit?" Abi raised her head and saw the Surgeon looking down at her. "You look as though you've seen an evil spirit!" Abi shuddered. "You look quite pale, my lad. Are you seasick?" Abi nodded dumbly. "What you need is a dose of *aqua menthe*," the Surgeon said kindly, opening his sturdy medicine chest and bending to examine the top tray. "Yes, here it is," he said, uncorking a small white jar. He sniffed. "That will sort out your ague." If he guessed there'd been any trouble, he didn't say.

Abi grimaced, expecting a foul-tasting brew, but the liquid was warm and smooth on her tongue. It smelled and tasted of mint. She felt it spreading down towards her stomach, and was comforted by it.

For a brief moment, she again wondered if she had been wise to run away from home. But now she was here, she had a problem to solve. If Master Pole was guilty, she must make sure he was found out – somehow.

The weather was still stormy, and Abi was soon too busy to worry about

being homesick. But she was terrified of encountering Piers again, and every time she was sent to help look after the wounded men on deck, she expected him to find her. Once, when Adam tapped her on the shoulder and asked her to fetch more bandages, she almost cried out.

# Tom

It was after noon the next day when Tom, Abi, Adam and the Surgeon landed on the quay at Portsmouth, shopping for fresh supplies.

"Follow me," said the Surgeon, disappearing into the mass of people milling about on the waterside. Tom, Abi and Adam pushed after him through the crowd, their legs unstable after so many days at sea. It was low tide, and down on the edge of the Camber they saw women and children collecting seaweed, seemingly unaware of the thick mud splashing up on to their clothes.

The Surgeon walked on and on, and Tom despaired of their ever stopping for something to eat. His stomach groaned as they turned into the high street and passed a baker's shop, but the Surgeon was heading into a narrow alley.

"Water, sweet water!" bawled a loud voice. They saw a water carrier in a blue woollen jacket and leather breeches, with his huge wooden scuttle over one shoulder. He strode into the alleyway from the street, pushing Abi out of the way. The Surgeon swung round, instantly alert. "Ah," he said. "Where he goes, we shall follow." Adam and Abi looked as puzzled as Tom felt, but they obediently followed the Surgeon. A few minutes later, he halted. "Told you," he said triumphantly, although he hadn't actually told them anything. "Wherever that man goes, we shall find people."

"But why do we want to find people?" Abi asked, mystified.

"It's always the way," the Surgeon said knowingly. "Where there's water for sale, there will be people – and they will probably be talking about

their ailments. It's a good place to gossip when you collect your water for the day. And where there are people talking about their ailments, an apothecary will set up shop. When one person is ill, others are soon persuaded. You'll see." He tipped his head back and laughed, sharing his joke with Abi. Tom scowled, jealous of the way the Surgeon gave his sister so much attention.

Two hours later they were on their way again, their stomachs filled at a nearby pastrycook's shop. Tom was pleased to be on the move; Abi bored him silly with her talk of medicines, and it had been hot and sweaty in the apothecary's shop.

"You have to be very careful with these, Tom," she had said knowingly, as she packed bottles containing small, round pills into her bag. "That ointment's *unguentum Egyptiacum*," she bragged, though struggling with the strange sounds of the Latin words. "Surgeon Spencer says it contains honey and vinegar in a beeswax base, and we use it to treat ulcers." She dropped several more containers into her bag, while Tom turned away to watch the bubbling mixtures in the tall glass bottles next to the furnace, and an apprentice pounding herbs in a metal mortar. The shop had been full of mysterious, intoxicating smells that had made him feel quite sleepy.

The Surgeon gave them permission to look round the market for an hour or two, "though make sure you're back on board by the tolling of the lookout watch; the light will be going by then." Carrying his share of the purchases, he ambled off down a side alley.

The three paused, and then turned to follow their sense of smell. In Baker's Lane, they found a heady mixture of odours: the scent of freshly baked bread, the strong stink of wet fish waiting to be bought. As they moved through the crowds into the Shambles Market, the mouth-watering smell of succulent roasting pig conquered the last vestiges of the cold, fresh sea air. For a while they forgot the ship, and wandered freely.

Tom stopped to look at some wood carvings on a stall, watching a bent old man in his leather apron at work on a piece of oak. After a moment he turned to talk to Abi, only to find that she'd moved on. Then he saw her: trust a girl! Abi, totally unaware of him, was immersed in a private dream. She was holding up lengths of Flanders lace, measuring them against her body as she'd done for Mistress de Vere. The stallholder had his back to her, interested only in gossiping, otherwise he would surely have chased off such a small, grubby boy . . .

Then Tom's heart missed a beat. A few yards away, on the edge of a crowd, stood Piers Jolland. He was watching Abi. Without thinking further, Tom barged past Piers, banging against him and shouting, "Stop, thief!" as loudly as he could. He waved his arms in the dusk, knocking off the hat of a passer-by. "Stop him, someone!" he shouted urgently. Then he plunged away into the shadows as other people took up the cry: "Stop, thief!" Tom was desperately hoping that Piers would be drawn along with the crowd, which was now pounding after him.

He worked out the lie of the land as he ran. It couldn't be far to the Camber ... He tore round to his right, past the church and into a narrow side street. There he stopped abruptly, falling back against the wooden perimeter fence of the graveyard. He waited for the thumping in his chest to stop as the rabble poured down to the waterfront, their cheering and whooping carrying far beyond the thudding of their feet. It wouldn't take them long to realise that they'd been duped.

Tom made his way round the edge of the graveyard and into St Thomas' Street. Then he went down a narrow alley on the north side of the church, where he could see only a small gap of sky between the jutting upper storeys of the houses. At last, he reached the Market Square once more – and there was Abi, looking lost. Adam had completely disappeared.

Cautiously, he crossed the square towards his sister, jumping over the gutter which was completely choked with stinking debris.

"Brother Kit," he said pointedly. "Piers has been watching from the other side of the square, and I'm not sure he knows what to make of you handling this lace with such ease!" He could see realisation grow in her face, and then shame and embarrassment.

"What was I thinking of? Tom, help me – what shall I do?" whispered Abi. "Where's Adam?"

"I don't know. Don't look round – just act naturally. At all costs, we must be gone before Piers finds his way back."

"We've got to get on board, don't forget," she hissed. "How are we going to manage that? He's bound to catch us up."

They turned, and started back towards the *Mary Rose*. A chill breeze had blown up, and as the dusk began to deepen they realised how late it must be. Not only was Piers a problem, but they would be in trouble with the Surgeon. Tom didn't want to let the old man down; he'd been good to them.

In the fading light, on the opposite side of the Camber, stood the round stone tower which guarded the entrance to the harbour. They could hear the continual wash and hiss of the sea as it foamed against the shore. The smell of wood smoke crept through the salt air as the townsfolk cooked their suppers, and Tom shivered from the chill of the oncoming night.

## Abi

As she and Tom retraced their steps to the ship, Abi turned to look back at the town. She gasped. There, no more than fifty paces away, stood Piers. He hadn't seen them. But there was no mistaking him, with his arrogant stance and his over-wide breeches. He looked rather like a cockerel. At any other time she would have chuckled, enjoying his ridiculous image, but now ... She turned to warn Tom, but he had already seen him.

As they watched, Piers strode briskly towards the landing stage. They backed away hastily, expecting that at any moment he would see them and catch hold of them. But he was clearly expecting a ship's boat to collect him, and within a short space of time, he started forward and stepped down out of sight. Abi could hear the cries of the lead boatman, and soon a ship's boat became visible as it set off towards the Mary Rose. Out in the bay, she watched the four great ships shifting with the flow of the tide, their night lanterns just tiny blobs of light.

For a moment, relief that Master Jolland had gone masked the fact that they were now stranded. But Tom was quick to point out the reality. Adam and the Surgeon would have been ferried back hours ago, and Piers had used the one remaining boat. "So it looks as if we will have a night in the open," he said. "And when we do get back to the ship, there's not exactly going to be a welcome party. Last time one of the boys was late back, before you joined the Mary Rose, they stripped him, strapped him to one of the guns and beat him 'til he bled."

Abi stood still, horrified, "But what if they do that to me, Tom ...?" She felt sick. She just couldn't imagine what would happen. She knew that the pain of being beaten would be bad enough – Pa had often taken a leather strap to her – but when they found out that she was a girl ... She just couldn't imagine being discovered in front of all those men.

She held back her fear. She wouldn't give way. Together, they stood watching the Mary Rose until the darkness was complete. It was getting colder and colder. They had nowhere to shelter, not much in the way of thick clothing to keep them warm, and nothing to eat.

They found an upturned boat propped against the round tower, and crawled underneath it. If it rained or even snowed, they would have some protection, but Abi had decided within a few minutes that sitting on cobbles was the most uncomfortable thing she could think of. The cold crept up through her breeches and numbed her right

through. Yes, there were definitely times when she missed being a normal girl living a normal life in a cottage!

# Tom

Tom woke suddenly a few hours later. His neck and back hurt, and for a moment he couldn't think where he was. Then it all flooded back. It was still pitch black under the boat, but he could hear a faint sound. That must have been what had made him stir. He turned awkwardly to pull himself out from under the boat, into the cold, clear air.

The sound was louder now: it was the gentle plash of oars bringing a boat towards them. Tom crossed his fingers, and hoped that whoever it was was friendly!

"Abi, wake up!" he hissed, poking his head back under the boat. "I think somebody's come for us." Then he ran to the landing. In the thinning grey of pre-dawn he could make out the shapes. Three people. And then he heard Adam's voice.

The boat swung up to the steps, and Tom dashed down to grab the rope. But the steps were slippery with mud and he lost his footing, almost plunging down into the water. Adam reached out and caught him. "Where on earth did you get to?" he demanded. "One minute you were there, and the next thing I knew, you were running straight into Piers and then tearing down the street like a madman! I tried to keep up, but then I lost you, so I came back and met up with the Surgeon."

Abi appeared at the top of the steps, still sleepy.

"Come on!" Tom's voice was angry, to cover up his embarrassment at slipping like that. Abi looked too much like a girl now, he thought; luckily, her cap had stayed on. "They've come to collect us." He moved into the prow of the boat to give her room to board. Tiny Henty the lookout boy held one oar, ready to pass it to Adam, and Martin held the other. "I can't say why I did that, Adam. I'm sorry," he said at last.

He stared intently at his cousin, willing him to understand. "But it was really important."

"What d'you mean, you can't say?" Martin muttered grumpily. "I get dragged out of my sleep by Adam and Henty here, and forced to row right across the harbour on an empty stomach – and then you turn round and tell us you can't say why!"

"Can't we just get back to the ship?" wailed Abi. "I'm so cold!" She shivered.

"Well, you would be – you're only a girl," squeaked tiny Henty, looking slyly across at her.

Tom, Abi and Adam froze. Martin looked so startled that Tom felt he might fall backwards into the water. "What the – don't talk rubbish!" said Adam sternly.

"How could he be on board if ..." Tom started to say.

But Henty held up his hands to quell their voices. "I know Kit's a girl!" he chortled in triumph. His thin chest jutted forward and his face grew as red as his tatty cap; he knew he was making an impact. "I overheard you two talking," he said, indicating the twins. "And *he* knows as well!" He pointed at Adam. "For all he's pretending now."

Martin gulped. "Are you?" was all he could manage. The sky was lightening, and the expressions on their faces were clearer now. Tom was interested to see that Abi looked shy as Martin spoke to her – unusual for her!

The convoy of ships had set sail for Boulogne. Sir Thomas Seymour had come on board. He was even more important than the Captain.

Only a day had passed since their wary return to the ship, but surprisingly, the Surgeon had been so pleased to see them safe and

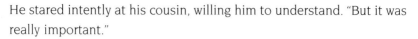

well that they'd escaped punishment. "I'm beginning to rely on you, Kit," was all he said, but it was enough to make Tom feel peeved. Still, at least they were back on board. And this was what he really loved: to be out on the busy open deck in the worst of the weather. Abi was welcome to the Surgeon's chest.

The sky darkened as though it were dusk, although it was still only the start of the forenoon watch. Black storm clouds towered overhead like an ugly giant, and the *Mary Rose* lifted and sank, waves crashing across her deck. The bulky form of Amos Wroth, the ship's Master, could be seen in his drenched doublet on the poop, solid as a rock as Tom lurched towards him.

"What the devil d'you think you're doing up here, boy?" hollered the Master in his no-nonsense voice. "You'll be washed overboard, and that'll be the end of you!"

"How far have we sailed, sir? Where are we?" Tom gasped as a strong gust of wind fisted him in the face.

"Oh, it's Master you'd be, is it?" Amos growled, but Tom could see the twinkle in his eye. "We've left the Isle of Wight a good three hours since, and we're crossing the seas to France – to a town called Boulogne on the northern coast." He pulled Tom back as a wave swept over the deck. "Come with me." Together, they crept to the ladder and felt their way down to the lower deck to find a little more shelter.

There was a pause while the Master turned away to watch some seamen putting extra lashings round the guns. "But as to why we're doing this, young man ...'Tis the King's will, and therefore God's, that we fight against King Francis. England and France are never friends for long. These kings always want more land than they've got. And if we don't win more of France, they're just as likely to try to capture a bit of English land."

The Master shook his head knowingly, and looked up at the steely grey sky. The wind howled round the empty masts; all the sails were tightly

furled against the spars to stop them being torn to shreds. "I've fought in many a battle against the French – and for the moment, His Majesty is more friends with the King of Spain. It seems it's either us or them. We still have hold of Calais, but we used to have hold of a great deal more. And the French pirates are forever raiding our ports."

"What will we do when we reach Boulogne?" Tom struggled with the unfamiliar name.

"Capture it, of course! Now, that's enough. Get below, young Master."

Tom looked at the murky sea ahead. For all he knew, the other ships might have reached Boulogne by now. He turned to go in through the stern arch, all the hatches being battened down, but as he reached for the door, a great wave swept over the deck, catching him and dragging him along in its wake.

He flung his arms out, grabbing at a gun as the water forced him along. He opened his mouth to shout, but choked on the rush of salt water. At last he managed to crawl into the shelter of the half-deck, where he found a ladder down to the gun deck. Feeling his heart thumping with the excitement of it all, he lowered himself down rung by rung.

The wind had abated somewhat and Tom had borrowed Adam's spare jerkin, but water still dripped down his neck. Only an hour ago he had been talking to the Master of the ship, feeling himself part of it all and riding out the rough sea … Now here he was, on guard for Abi on the gun deck. He was trying to look casual and busy at the same time, while all round him, seamen were cleaning the decks or tying ropes more securely.

His belly was taut with nerves because Abi was breaking into Pole's cabin. Working with the Surgeon seemed to set him apart a little, and nobody bothered to question his reason for standing there.

Tom flexed his leg muscles and forced himself to breathe deeply. Once again, for about the hundredth time, he cast his eyes round the deck and as far as he could see up the steps to the open deck. If Henry Pole suddenly appeared, it was his responsibility to get Abi out of danger. That was the plan, but he was less than convinced that it was workable.

# Abi

A thrill ran down Abi's spine. She crept over to the officers' cabins, opposite the Surgeon's cabin. Surely it wouldn't take long to search – a cabin was more like a stable than a proper room. Just enough room to pack in a bunk and a chest. She felt quite sick. It was so dark; only one lantern swung here. Her legs felt weak. How could she be doing this? The third door. That was the cabin she'd been in when Pole called for his medicine just a few days ago.

There was no one around to watch her movements, but that made it even more dangerous. If Pole suddenly appeared, she would have no hope of escape, no reason for being there. She crept forward a few more paces – more than she intended as the ship surged forward. She was rushed down the passageway and then, like it or not, she was at his door.

Taking a deep breath, Abi reached out and pushed the sliding door to one side. Unlike the last time, it moved quite freely. Two steps and she was in. No time to stop and think. Hastily she scanned the cabin, choking back a wave of nerves she realised what she had got herself into. She stepped over to the officer's chest. She had just enough room to slip between the bunk and the chest.

She lifted the lid and felt for the tray. With every move she made, the possibility of escape and freedom became less likely. If Pole came in now, he could quite rightly have her hanged for stealing. As carefully as she could, she felt the layers of clothing, trying to identify each item by touch. There was very little light – only the weak beams filtering

through the doorway and the cracks in the boarding from the lantern in the passageway. She could hardly breathe with anticipation, she was so nervous. But she had to keep going. If he was guilty, there had to be a way of getting him punished.

At length, she gave up. It was quite obvious that there were no boots in the chest. All that risk for nothing. Her heart sank. The thought that maybe she'd been wrong flitted across her mind – but no. She had thought he was a brute the first time she came across him in Lavenham; now, she was convinced he was evil.

Faintly, then louder, she heard Tom's voice. He was calling her. She couldn't hear what he was saying, but never mind. He must be warning her that Pole was in sight. Abi leaped to her feet, her heart thumping painfully in the back of her throat. She flung the tray back into place and swung round towards the doorway. And then, out of the corner of her eye, she saw them. Sticking out from under a rough blanket on the bunk. The toes of the red boots!

Abi ran through the doorway and fled to the safety of the gun deck. A hand caught her arm, and she all but shrieked out loud, but then she heard Tom's voice in her ear. Master Pole appeared, moving towards his cabin from the entrance to the forecastle. Without looking at him, the twins slipped down the steps to the orlop deck.

The *Mary Rose* bucked as her gunners fired their first broadside. The battle had begun. Abi picked herself up from the deck where she'd fallen, and stood still, listening. She and Tom had been waiting for the inevitable injured seamen, but now she couldn't hear anything.

When it came, the noise was horrifying. Abi had never heard anything like it. All thoughts of her close escape from Pole flew from her mind – time enough for that later. Down here, the air was thickening with

smoke from the guns. Abi's eyes watered, and she dragged the back of her hand across them. The reek of gunpowder set her coughing. Then Tom appeared, and Abi giggled. "Have you seen your face?" she shrieked, gazing in amazement at the black streaks round his eyes.

"No, but have you seen yours?" he retorted, laughing.

"Out of my way!" A gunner with a grimy face shoved the twins clear as he and three others threw their full weight at a big gun on its carriage, pushing it to the open gun port. Then the man bent over to pick up a long wooden linstock, with a hand-carved end like the face of a dragon. He jammed a slow match into its mouth, held it to the touch hole and stepped quickly out of the way.

This time Abi was prepared, holding her hands tightly over her ears, waiting for the explosion. The bang seemed to lift the top of her head off. The huge bronze gun squealed back as two seamen leaped clear to avoid losing their feet. Another man ran to sponge the gun out, then thrust a staff with a lambskin mop on the end down the vent. All round Abi, these men seemed completely immersed in their own world. It was as though she was invisible; and the smoke was so dense that it was almost impossible to recognise anyone down here. She coughed as the powder caught in her throat, and wondered if anything would ever be normal again.

Behind them, a man shrieked in agony. Abi was at his side before Tom had even turned round. "What's happened?" she demanded, but no answer was needed, as she saw blood gushing down the man's cheek. He clutched his hands and doubled up in pain.

"Come with me," she said softly, keen to help him. But the seaman ignored her, groaning and writhing as his mates turned back to work their gun. Abi tried to tug the man to his feet and along the deck towards the stern, but he was so heavy – at least twice her weight. Then, in the nick of time, Tom joined her, and together they guided the man through the smoke and guns to the Surgeon's cabin.

"What's wrong with you, good fellow?" Surgeon Spencer forced the man's hands away from his face to reveal a large splinter embedded in his cheek. "Hmmm. Give me my small knife," he said to no one in particular.

Abi sprang to attention, and confidently picked out a bone-handled blade. Adam appeared from nowhere to pinion the man's muscular arms tightly behind him, while the Surgeon deftly cut the flesh away from the spike of wood.

For what seemed like eternity, the guns continued to fire. It was some time later that Abi realised she could speak without having to shout, and hear without straining her ears. Then it was time to swab the decks and clear away all the bandages. She realised that she was ravenously hungry – since the early forenoon, she had eaten nothing.

Darkness clung around the ship. Lanterns lurched and spiralled from the deck heads like dizzy moths as the *Mary Rose* continued on her way. All around Abi, men slept on the deck like the dead bodies they'd "buried" over the side earlier in the day.

But Abi remained wide awake. In the peace after the battle, she was worrying about Henry Pole. Was there a connection between Edward Ferris's death and Lavenham? Or was it a coincidence? She needed to know.

Surgeon Spencer moved past silently in his cut-fingered shoes, stooping to check the wounded. Abi had helped him as much as possible, but Tom, with equal enthusiasm, had kept himself out of sight. She felt in her pocket, drew out a biscuit hoarded from their last meal, and broke off a piece to stow in her mouth. After a while it would soften a little, and she would suck off the outer edges and chew it. She

preferred eating ship's biscuits in the dark. The weevils didn't taste so bad when you couldn't see them. They were just a bit cold, like jelly.

Her head began to nod in time to the motion of the ship. She was so tired. With luck they'd be back in Portsmouth soon. And then she'd have to do something ... her head dropped a little lower ... she'd have to tell Adam and Martin that she'd seen the red boots ...

# Tom

Tom listened to his sister as, yet again, she worked through her thoughts about Henry Pole. The twins, Adam and Martin were all crammed into Martin's cabin, although it was even smaller than Pole's. He had to share it with the Quartermaster; one of them slept while the other was on duty.

The ship was back at anchor outside the harbour at Portsmouth, and for once, no one seemed to want to issue orders. The great ship drifted calmly on its anchor chain.

"What if Henry Pole has been blackmailing Master de Vere?" Adam whispered suddenly. He turned to include Martin. "At home in Lavenham."

"Why?" Abi jumped in before Tom could open his mouth. "Blackmailing him about what?"

Adam lowered his voice even further so that Tom could hardly hear him. "Master de Vere and his wife have remained with the old faith," he said.

Tom heard a sharp intake of breath from Abi. He cut in quickly this time, before his twin could speak. "You mean they're still following the Mass and the P – I mean the Bishop of Rome?" (Pa still called him "the Pope" out of habit, but that was dangerous since King Henry had outlawed being Catholic, in favour of his new 'Church of England'.)

"Exactly!"

"What do you think he's after then – money?" Martin pondered.

Adam turned to the older boy. "Well if that was the case, it would be easy. The de Veres are rich – no, there's got to be something else to make Master Pole and Master de Vere have such rows."

"What about Edward Ferris? How does he fit into all this?" Tom put the question in hesitantly. He always seemed to be the last to work out the connections, and he didn't want to look a fool now.

"Good question, young Tom," said Adam. "Well, the only thing I can think of is Mistress Mary de Vere."

"The de Veres' daughter?"

"And you think that Pole took a fancy to the daughter?" Martin butted in unexpectedly. "Well, there's nothing wrong with that. Pole has been brought up to be a citizen in the town, even though his family are only yeomen farmers."

Adam nodded his head in agreement, so that Tom felt left out again. "Mistress Mary doesn't like him, although she's known him all her life. After young Master Roger died, Pole used to look after her and take her out riding. But whenever he turns up, she disappears to her room and stays there. I know because I've had to take meals up to her."

"But what are we going to do about it?" Abi burst in. "Won't Master de Vere be executed if he's discovered following Popish ways?" she hissed, struggling to keep her voice down. "And that still doesn't tell us why Master Pole killed Edward Ferris."

"He might be executed," Martin said quietly. "It might depend on whether he holds any office for the King. He's not in the same position as Archbishop Cranmer – it's ten years now since *he* lost his head – but the de Veres are certainly breaking the law, and the more wealth you have, the more noticeable you are."

Around them, the ship creaked; it seemed to be holding its breath and listening to their words. Then Adam looked up. "Got it!" he said. "The

last time Pole came to the house, he had a man with him. I didn't take much notice; I don't think anyone did. The only one who reacted was Mary, because I saw them ride up and I was able to warn her so that she could make her usual move upstairs. That would have been the time when your Ma died." He paused, embarrassed, looking at Abi. Tom sensed that he was leading up to something important. "In our first few days on board, I kept wondering why Master Ferris's face was so familiar. Now I know . . ."

"You mean, it was Ferris who visited the de Veres with Pole?" Martin's voice caught in excitement.

"Yes, and not only did Pole row with Master de Vere, but he also yelled at Master Ferris. In fact, it seemed to be one long row: first with Master de Vere, then, as I was sweeping the floor in the hallway, Pole walked in and threatened this other man. I can't remember his words exactly, but it was something to do with being loyal ... and what Ferris thought Pole paid him for. He was really mad. He smashed his fist down hard on the table and made the fruit bowl bounce." Adam flinched at the memory. "I was in the room, but you know what they're like, these people educated above their station – I might as well have been one of the chairs. Yes, it's all coming back to me now. He said, 'I will marry Mistress Mary if it's the last thing I do!'"

Adam sat back, flushed, and Tom sneaked a look outside the cabin to make sure no one had overheard. They had all been so intent on the conversation that anyone could have crept up and they wouldn't have noticed. But no one was there.

"So what you're saying," Martin said, counting points off on his fingers, "is that Henry Pole was close to the de Veres – after the only son died, he spent quite a lot of time looking after the only daughter – yes?" Adam nodded. "As he got older, he realised that he might be able to make something out of his efforts, and he asked to marry Mistress Mary . . ."

"Master de Vere said no," Abi butted in, unable to keep silent any longer. "And Mary didn't want to marry Pole anyway."

"And then Henry Pole started blackmailing the family because he knew they were still active Catholics! Edward Ferris used to work for Pole, but he was a good man, and when he realised what his master was up to, he threatened to make things difficult for him," Adam finished with a flourish.

Tom knew that Martin was making a decision. "I'm the eldest here, and I say we wait before we do anything – particularly as we have other problems." Martin glanced at Abi, and Tom was amused to see her blush. "Pole can't go anywhere while we're at sea, and we need time to think."

Abi shook her head. "He mustn't get away with it! But how can we go to the Captain? He'd never believe our word against Henry Pole's."

Tom, Abi, Adam and Martin were waiting for Piers on the gun deck. They were going into Portsmouth to help the Lord Mayor's men prepare for the Christmas feasting. Tom felt a burst of excitement welling up inside him as Henry Pole strode out from under the half-deck and went straight over to the tumblehome.

"Hope he falls in!" muttered Adam, glancing across at his cousin to see her smile.

When Piers arrived, they had to climb down the steep side of the ship. Abi took one look at the waves slopping about in the gap between the two vessels, closed her eyes, and leaped out and down. She landed clumsily in the bottom of the ship's boat, and grabbed at the side to steady herself. It was only the second time she'd been off the *Mary Rose* in six weeks.

The oarsmen started pulling towards the busy dock, and gradually

they drew away from the ship. The motion was much jerkier in such a small boat, and a biting cold breeze hit them as they left the shelter of the *Mary Rose*. Once Piers was settled in the prow and out of earshot, Adam turned his back on him. "I can't believe that anyone could be so ruthless. Can you imagine marrying the daughter of the man you're blackmailing?"

"And telling Mistress Mary that he could get her father killed!" said Abi. "He's a monster! He makes Piers seem almost normal." Tom chuckled, and Abi grinned across at him.

"Well, you know what I mean," she said. "The idea of what he's done makes my blood boil."

The boat reached the quay, and swung round to bang against the stonework. Piers leaped out and up the steep steps – it was all they could do to keep up with their lanky leader. They hurried along the northern bank of the Camber and past the squat Chantry Chapel. Close to the water, a square tower loomed into focus. As they walked in the clear frosty air, they could see right across the sea to the distant outline of the Isle of Wight.

The great wooden door was opened to admit them, and they pushed inside. At once they were aware of the warmth and the brightness of the rush lamps, compared to the continual dullness of the ship. They were shown to the banqueting hall, where a long wooden table stood on a dais. When the linen cloths were in place, the five of them started helping the Mayor's servants to set out the enormous feast. The room seemed large and welcoming after the confined areas of the ship, although it wasn't grand. Behind the hastily hung tapestries, Tom noticed that the walls were plain brick.

After a while, the door opened and Henry Pole came in. He stood quietly, watching them. Tom noticed that Abi couldn't keep her eyes off him. He didn't even appear to have noticed her as an individual, yet she kept as far away from him as possible. He seemed to have an

aura of menace about him, and the boy couldn't help noticing that Piers was watching him, too.

As it neared the time for the Mayor and his guests to arrive, the food was brought in. There were large platters of juicy meats: roast beef, brawns and jellies scooped from the boar's neck, mutton, venison, and, in the middle of it all, the roasted boar's head garlanded with rosemary. Tom felt as if he was in paradise. Never in his life had he seen so much food. The smells of the cooked meat were so mouth-watering; he almost felt as if he was eating the fine food himself.

A great fire in the hearth was continuously fed with enormous logs, and light from the flames shot dancing shadows into the corners of the hall. For the first time in weeks, Tom felt warm.

Martin had poured them each a glass of mead, and they'd hurriedly drunk it in the shadow of a pillar before anyone spotted them. The mellow aftertaste rested pleasantly in Tom's mouth, and the tension that had persisted since Abi's arrival began to leave him. The more he thought about that meat, the more his stomach rumbled. There was meat on the ship, of course, but it was often cold by the time it was his turn.

Piers was everywhere, bullying them to get all the platters laid and the branches of holly decked across the bare parts of the walls. Tom was aware of the Steward's assistant scowling at them, but he didn't seem so threatening now. Abi seemed a bit restless – he noticed that she was slipping further and further away from him – but so what? He felt a grudging respect for how well she'd done since she'd joined the *Mary Rose*.

## Abi

As the musicians took their places in the high gallery and the Mayor's guests began to arrive, Abi was aware of Piers at her side. She tried to

shuffle away, but whenever she sidestepped, Piers moved with her. Suddenly, he shot out his arm, took hold of her and pulled her behind a screen. "I want some information from you!" he whispered. Abi was too stunned to say anything. She waited to see what would come next. "I want to know what *you* know about red boots."

Piers' face swam in close to hers. He had her by both arms now, and she could smell the ale on his breath. Why did it matter so much to him? He seemed desperate, and she didn't know what to do. She tried to look round for Tom, but Piers was holding her tightly. "If you don't tell me, you will be well and truly sorry."

Abi's mind froze. She couldn't think of anything to say. She stared up at Piers as defiantly as she could.

And then she heard the Captain's voice. The music had stopped, and from the main part of the hall she heard Captain Grenville saying, "Master Jolland's new servants will do …." A pulse began to throb in Abi's neck, and she was aware that Piers was not at ease, either. "Those twins can dance for us. Where are they?" The Captain's voice was moving towards them. Piers sighed and pulled Abi into the main part of the hall.

## Tom

Tom saw Piers pull Abi out from behind a screen. But he had no time to wonder what was happening, for Henry Pole, who had never spoken a word to him, suddenly loomed up in front of him and shoved him out on to the open floor.

Captain Grenville, a tall, powerful man in a dark-violet coat and green breeches, swaggered up to Tom, his glass of mead in his hand. "Yes, these twins can entertain us," he chuckled in a light-hearted, teasing manner, "and one of them will have to play the lady."

A chorus of cheers met this pronouncement, and Tom felt the

attention of the crowd focusing on him. A drop of sweat crept inside the lining of his collar and down his spine as he forced a smile. It was all very well for the Captain to joke, but he didn't know the serious consequences of the joke going wrong.

"Who's the more handsome, eh?" The Captain turned to catch Abi under the chin and tilt her face up towards the firelight. Around them, the ribald comments and laughter grew louder. Tom flinched in horror. This couldn't be happening, soon he must wake to the rocking motion of the ship . . . But the nightmare continued.

Abi could dance. That was the problem. She could dance very well, given that she was no lady. Adam had taught her when they had all been working in the de Veres' household. But how could she pretend to be the girl and yet appear boyish – when she *was* a girl? Tom's head swam.

"Musicians – play us an almaine!" The Mayor gestured at the four men up on their balcony. Even they were hanging over the balustrade and laughing. Hastily, they grabbed their instruments and launched into a fast dance tune. The crowd fell back, leaving Tom and Abi in the middle of the floor.

"Shall you be the girl, Tom? And I'll be the boy?" Abi's cheeks had paled, and Tom had never seen her look so scared. He squeezed her cold fingers gently. Behind them, someone belched and sniggered.

Together, they "simpled" and "doubled" in circles and stepped and hopped in almaine fashion, cautiously to start with, but then with more and more confidence. The room swung round them, and Tom relaxed a little. He began to enjoy showing off.

So did Abi. She smiled across at him, and a sense of wellbeing and exultation swept through him like fire. Here they were, hundreds of miles from home, working on King Henry's famous ship. He was here with his sister, whom he loved best in the world – and no one knew their secret!

Then it happened. It was after a circle, when the steps of the man and the lady were identical. Before he could stop himself, Tom swept Abi into the lady's position, sloping his right arm out and round as he'd seen Master de Vere do, and Abi automatically responded. He faltered, horrified as Abi's eyes met his, realising what they had done. The whole world stopped – but two dozen pairs of eyes still watched. Even the music seemed to be hovering, holding its breath. Waiting.

# Abi

Slowly, nonchalantly, Abi shrugged, while her heart pounded. It was too late to change back now. She continued to dance the lady's part while her mind raced ahead. She imagined she could feel Piers' eyes following her everywhere, his suspicion growing. Surely everyone would spot the difference, her ease in the lady's position . . .

From another direction, she became conscious of someone else watching her, and she felt herself blushing. Since Henty's spluttered announcement in the boat, Martin had been different towards her, softening his voice when he spoke to her. Nothing much, but enough to show that he liked her, and she was beginning to depend on his liking.

The dance ended in a storm of clapping and shouting for more. Abi stood rooted to the spot, still holding her brother's hand and wondering what to do next.

Then Martin stepped forward with a flourish. He doffed his cap and turned to an astonished Piers. "Would you care for the next dance, m'lady?" he asked loudly.

Piers looked stunned, and then haughty. "I don't play the fool!" he spat out.

"Oh, yes, you do, Master Jolland," came the smooth tones of the Captain. With bad grace, Piers snatched Martin's hand and moved out on to the floor, as the crowd around them guffawed in delight.

# Tom

By God's grace, the new year of 1545 was four weeks old, and still Abi was surviving as a boy. Her hair was growing longer again – she'd have to watch that, thought Tom – but the weather had been so bad that no one took their clothes off. No one even considered washing. Piers continued to watch her, trying to catch her alone.

Tom shivered. The dank atmosphere pervaded the whole ship. But at least they were off again. They were about to sail in convoy with the great Admiral de Lisle in command, and there was a sense of anticipation on board. The flagship was the "Great Harry" (as the Master affectionately called her). Her proper name was the *Henri Grace à Dieu*.

From the Captain's cabin, Tom heard the muffled shouts of the Master and his mates. Whistles blew and the ship creaked as the anchor was hauled up out of the mud and the ship swung into the wind.

He noticed the dim shapes of the square tower and the buildings on the far side of the Camber. In his mind's eye, he could see the way the land folded back as they ran along the coast. How the new castle at Southsea dominated the landscape, and how, a long way inland, the hills rose to meet the sky. Ahead of the *Mary Rose*, the spread of the sea extended further and further, until, once they had left the shelter of the Isle of Wight, there was no more land to see. Just miles and miles of water. Tom breathed out, in his element once more.

The deck tilted, sending the bowls clattering across the Captain's table and stirring Tom from his daydream. He rushed to catch them before they crashed to the deck; before Piers could come and shout at him.

They were off to fight the French again, Amos Wroth had told him. Fears that they were building a powerful battle fleet were growing, and King Henry's fleet was to cross the Channel to raid and destroy King Francis' ships. They were heading for a port called Le Havre, where,

58

the Master guessed, the French fleet would be anchored. "We shall try to board their ships so we can steal them and use them ourselves, young Tom," he'd said, a glint of excitement at the thought of such a challenge showing in his weatherbeaten face. "And those we can't board, we shall set alight. Send a fireboat into their midst. Wouldn't want them invading us, would we?"

As swiftly as he could, Tom finished his tasks and slipped out to make his way up to the deck. Piers had still not appeared, and he was worried in case the Steward's assistant had succeeded in cornering his sister again.

# Abi

"That's settled!" The Surgeon stepped into his tiny cabin, where Abi was cleaning up, and flopped down on the narrow bench.

"What's settled, Surgeon?" Abi was curious. It was unlike him to show any enthusiasm for anything, although she knew he cared a great deal about the health of the men. It must be something important.

"*You* are settled, young Kit. I've been to Captain Grenville, and he's agreed." He paused, knowing that Abi would not be able to wait.

"Well? Agreed to what?"

"Simple!" The old man tossed one of his jars into the air so that it twisted and dropped into Abi's hand. "As soon as possible, you're to be indentured as my mate." Abi gasped in disbelief and excitement. "Mind you, the best bit about all this is that I've scored one over that good-for-nothing Master Piers Jolland!" The Surgeon chuckled in obvious delight. "It seems that he had told the Captain that you and Tom were his servants. Well, I soon set things right. Captain Grenville knows I need good people to work for me. He likes a healthy ship – and he never thought to ask if you'd been signed on. He wouldn't bother about such petty matters. Yes, go and tell that brother of

yours." He nodded at Abi, a comfortable smile on his face. "But he won't want the same, I'll be bound. He likes to be on deck too much." The Surgeon chuckled again, and Abi ran to climb the ladders to the open deck.

Whenever he had a free moment, Tom could be found up on deck with Amos Wroth, learning the arts of navigation.

Abi had no difficulty these days in moving with the motion of the ship, and as she reached Piers' cabin, she almost unconsciously skirted the sleeping bodies of the men who were off-watch. Two lads were playing nine-men's-morris on a board scraped into the top of a barrel, and scarcely looked up as she passed.

As always, she paused near Piers' door, trying to decide whether he was in there or not. She was just preparing to dash past when she heard a low, croaky voice from the other side of the door.

"You can write your promise on a scrap of parchment. Then I shall know you will honour it." That was Giles Elliott the Quartermaster! Abi edged closer, her curiosity getting the better of her. Although it was still afternoon, the gun deck was dark, and by leaning against the thin partition, she could quite safely listen without anyone bothering her.

The two men were talking more softly now, as though aware of her presence. By turning sideways, Abi found that she could see through a slit in the boarding. Piers had his back to her and was in shadow. Giles' hands, lit by the lantern overhead, were resting on a barrel top.

"All right, I'll scribe it." Piers sounded sulky. Then: "Make sure you keep this safe, Master Elliott, otherwise I'll end up in chains in the hold."

"Don't worry, Master Jolland, I have no intention of losing such a precious document, given as how Captain Grenville is so against gambling. This will bring me a tidy sum of money ..." He coughed. "It makes sure that you will pay me."

"I'll pay you. Just give me time," Piers spat out as he wrote.

For the last few seconds, Abi's heart had been thumping wildly. This was why he was so desperate for information, why he wanted to know what was so important to her about the red boots. After all, he, as Pole's assistant, would know that they belonged to his Master. He wanted to know if there was any information he could use against Pole, if Pole found out that he gambled. It sounded as though he had a big debt. This was it: this was how she could get Piers off her back. If she could only get hold of that scrap of parchment . . .

Without thinking further, she slid open the door to the tiny cabin and boldly grabbed the parchment from the barrel. Outside again, she paused, half-blinded by the candlelight in the cabin. Then she heard Piers' startled shout, and she was off.

She ran along the forward deck, jumping with more luck than judgement over sleeping bodies, and sprang up the step that told her she was under the forecastle. She raced for a hatch. She could hear Piers crashing along behind her, and she heard him trip up the same step.

She expected to be shouted at, and, after that first mad impulse, she couldn't quite see how she had expected to get away with it. The chase continued. She ran to the base of a ladder and pulled herself up to a scuttle hatch. Perhaps Piers was so scared of the Captain finding out about his gambling that he daren't risk drawing attention to her by shouting.

Still clutching the scrap of parchment and willing Tom to realise what was going on, Abi reached above her head and found the hatch separating the gun deck from the deck above. She pushed, and the hatch clattered free. Abi climbed up through the gap. There was easily enough room for her, but Piers would find it a tight fit. She dropped the hatch back into its place just as Piers reached the bottom of the ladder, and then she made for the open deck.

Her breath came in short gasps, and the cold salt air stung her lungs.

Looking around quickly to make sure that she was unobserved in the fading light, she stumbled across to starboard. There was only one way to go, and that was up! She spotted the Master and her brother on the half-deck, but although she wanted Tom to come and help her, she found herself moving across the deck towards the main mast. Piers' head appeared below her, and she slipped across the remaining decking.

Abi reached to grab at the main mast rigging, and then swung out and round. She didn't dare to look at the dark, tumbling mass of water below. Wooden rail in one hand, thick, tarred netting in the other. One slip and she would be dead.

Her head was whipped back by the wind and her cap blew off, but by some miracle she managed to grab it and stuff it down inside her jerkin. She would be frozen in no time. How Henty survived in his fighting top, she could not imagine. She took a deep breath and began to climb, holding the ropes so tightly that at times she could hardly let go to climb further. Up, and up, and up.

At one point she lost her footing and slipped. It was only by hanging from a rope by her arms that she stopped herself plunging to the deck. The rope burned her palms as it tore into her skin, and her feet grappled in the air until, at last, she found a footing and was able to carry on up.

Once, she looked down and thought she saw Piers watching from the shadows, but she couldn't be sure; she was no longer sure of anything. She was so cold that she almost fell asleep, but then she imagined Tom's voice, telling her to keep going.

She didn't pause until she saw the base of the first fighting top just above her. Then, thankfully, she crawled through the hole in the centre, to relative safety and a bit of shelter. She pulled herself up to a kneeling position – and met Henty's staring face.

Grinning, she pointed downwards and put a finger to her lips. Henty

grinned back, and nodded. Together, they leaned out over the wooden rim and peered at the dark shape of the deck. Far below, a figure detached itself from the forecastle, sloped across the deck and disappeared through the hatch to the main gun deck.

The ship surged onwards in the growing darkness. Then the ship's bell sounded for the watch to change. Minutes later, a face appeared through the lubbers' hole. Ignoring the boy's surprise at seeing Abi, she and Henty began their long descent to the deck.

As she swung downwards, striving to keep up with Henty's easy movements, she remembered that she'd stuffed the parchment in the back of her belt. What if it slipped out and was lost? Half-way down to the deck, she twisted her legs round a thick rope and hung with one hand while she tugged at the parchment with the other. But just before she could tuck it inside her jerkin, the wind whipped her prize out of her fingers and whirled it away into the night.

# Tom

By the time the French coast was sighted, the brief spell of good weather had ended, forcing the ships to straggle along in a ragged cluster. It was three days since reinforcements from the east coast of England had joined them.

The great buff sails of the other ships disappeared and reappeared as the *Mary Rose* lifted and dipped over each wave, and it was hard work for Tom to stay upright. Sometimes he could see the deck of the *Minion*; sometimes she all but disappeared. The *Peter* leaned in their direction at such an angle that Tom held his breath, waiting for the ship to keel over.

He clawed his way forward past clumps of crouching seamen, and in the shelter of the archway into the forecastle he leaned out over the side to watch the "Great Harry" tacking in front of them. At one point,

a pale shaft of sunlight broke through the clouds, lighting up the tiny gold orb and crown in the bows of the flagship. They stood alone on their own tiny mast on the bowsprit, upright and proud, as the great ship forged onwards towards the enemy.

The grey coastline of France grew more distinct by the hour. By noon, the mouth of a great river could be seen. The landscape was flat, and the horizon was a simple straight line. A large town sprawled round the bay: Le Havre, according to Martin. The wooden buildings of the town took shape as they sailed closer.

Tom's eyes watered in a puff of smoke drifting from the bows of the "Great Harry", and seconds later, he heard the bang of a ship's gun – although he couldn't work out what they were firing at. A second shot followed, and then a third.

In amazement, Tom made out the lines of a mass of low boats coming towards them, their oars lifting and falling in a blur. These must be the French galleys that Master Wroth had told him about. What he hadn't said was how long they were.

The galleys streamed out of the mouth of the river towards the English ships. There were dozens of them. They were low in the water, long and squat like water beetles. Hundreds of men sat in rows of five or six to an oar. To his horror, Tom saw the glint of metal on their raised arms as the sun broke through the clouds. They were slaves! Chained into position! If the galleys were sunk by the English guns, the men would go down without a chance to escape.

# Abi

Two decks below Tom, Abi closed the Surgeon's chest and scooped up the pile of pewter bowls and brass syringes, along with two sponges. She began to climb the stairway up to the main gun deck. It was difficult to manage everything, to hold on to the wooden rail while

balancing her load in her other hand. With her head down and the top of the pile wedged under her chin and against her chest, she crept upwards, pausing with each heave of the ship.

Without warning, a hand clamped down over her mouth, stifling her and pulling her backwards. Instinctively, Abi clutched at the ladder, but Piers' strength was too much for her and she felt herself being dragged down. The backs of her legs crashed painfully against the lower steps of the ladder, and her bowls and syringes bounced and rolled away across the deck.

"What have you done with it?" Piers growled. "I've been waiting to get my hands on you for three days, but you're always with your precious Surgeon."

Abi flinched. How could she answer if she couldn't open her mouth? Then it came to her. Piers didn't know she'd lost the parchment. He wouldn't know unless she told him. With difficulty, she opened her mouth and bit Piers' hand. It tasted revolting! The scent of musk must hide weeks of dirt and grime.

With a yell, Piers let his hand drop. He grabbed at Abi's wrist and kicked out viciously at her shins. Her legs buckled with pain, and she dropped to the deck. But then Piers hissed, "Shh – the guard!" Footsteps paced overhead, paused, and faded away. For a moment, the only sound was the groaning and creaking of the ship's timbers.

Abi shook herself free, rubbing her bruised legs. She tensed, expecting Piers to catch hold of her again. But no – she realised that he was waiting for her to speak. He needed to know about Pole – this seemed far more important to him than the parchment.

She decided to tell him – about being up on deck, about seeing the fight and about watching a man, whom she now knew to be Henry Pole, wearing his red boots, peering over the edge of the ship as the body of Edward Ferris drifted away into the dark. After all, Piers would

have a far greater chance of speaking to the Captain than she would. And he might be less brutal to her in the future ...

# Tom

Tom stared at the French galleys, unable to move as they came closer. They kept disappearing from sight behind the swelling waves.

Then the Master came up to him and nudged him into action. "Get below where you belong," he ordered. No time for friendly comments now. Gunshots sounded from the "Great Harry", and Tom ran aft under the shelter of the half-deck. He slipped down the hatch to the gun deck, and was reluctantly moving towards the Surgeon's cabin when a hand landed on his shoulder. He swung round to find Martin following him.

"Come into my cabin," he whispered. "I've already got Abi – I mean Kit."

Tom fell through the narrow doorway and flopped down on the bench bed.

"I'm not staying here all the time," Abi warned sternly, looking at Martin. Tom realised that, for the first time ever, he and his twin were having very different thoughts. With an even greater shock, he realised that his sister and Martin were holding hands. "When our guns start firing, I must go and help the Surgeon. Men will be wounded. I should go now." She started to stand up, but Martin pushed her gently back.

"Not yet," he said gruffly.

A deafening noise, like thunder, filled the air as the first of the *Mary Rose*'s guns fired. Then the heavy rumbling of wheels sounded a few feet away on the far side of the panelling.

Abi wriggled. "I'm going, and you can't stop me! I've got important work to do." She hauled back the flimsy door and threw a glance at Martin.

Tom watched her disappear into the jumble of bodies and shouting men. Another gun crashed its shot towards the enemy. Thick smoke rolled across the deck, and Tom coughed as the acrid tang caught the back of his throat.

"I suppose I'd better go as well," he sighed. Visions of bloodied limbs swam uncomfortably through his mind. He pulled himself through the narrow opening, but Abi was already out of sight. Then, as he neared a companion ladder amidships, he realised that something was wrong. Amos Wroth and the Captain were arguing up on deck.

"If we don't go about soon, we shall be grounded!" That was Amos, his voice clear above the shouts of the gunners. "These waters shelve too quickly for the likes of the *Mary Rose*."

"Admiral de Lisle has not tacked, and until he does, I can do nothing." The Captain was almost shouting as huge waves crashed against the hull.

Tom crept up a few rungs of the ladder until he could see their tense faces. Master Wroth did not tolerate fools, and the boy could read his face quite plainly. "So we shall just sail on to our doom because the good Lord hasn't seen fit to grant us a sane captain, eh?"

A voice sounded like a trumpet call from the bows: "Get the archers to their stations!" A group of men carrying longbows knocked Tom off the ladder in their haste to respond, while other archers tramped overhead. Tom climbed up the ladder again, straining to hear the conversation, but the two men had turned their backs.

"Master Wroth ... cannot allow talk ... well you know it." The Captain had lowered his voice, and his words flew with the wind. "I certainly trust your knowledge of these waters ... sailed them since you were a boy ... but I have no choice." Unexpectedly, the Captain turned, and his last sentence was unmistakable: "So long as the flagship continues on her course, I may not tack. It would be deemed treason if I did."

Tom hurried away to the Surgeon's cabin. What would happen if the *Mary Rose* ran aground? He had no idea at all. Would she sink? Would she topple over? Would they all drown?

His nostrils picked up the sickly smell of burned flesh. In what seemed like a tiny hell, he watched Abi calmly smearing ointment on a livid red powder burn. She helped the man to his feet and patted him on the back as he stumbled through to the deck. Tom had just opened his mouth to offer his help when the ship shuddered.

The galleys had fired a hit! But how? Then he remembered. He'd hardly registered it at the time. They had guns, large ones, in the bows. All they had to do was to row up and fire under the sprit sail into the main part of the ship. Amos Wroth's voice came quite clearly to mind. "Galleys can do a lot of damage, young Tom, and it's difficult for us in our big ships to stop them. It's the guns, you see – our guns are trained to fire on other ships of our own size. Our guns aim too high to hit the galleys." Perhaps he needn't feel so sorry for those slaves.

A second shudder followed, and then a third, before the *Mary Rose* returned the fire. The deck kicked back with the force of the gunshots, and then fell away as a huge wave cannoned against the hull. Somewhere on the upper deck, a man screamed.

Giles the Quartermaster appeared at Tom's shoulder. "Where's the Surgeon?" he rasped. The little man popped out of his cabin. "Surgeon – come quickly, if you please. Francis Medley has his leg trapped beneath a gun. The carriage overturned ..." Before Giles had finished speaking, Tom found himself holding armfuls of bandages. The Surgeon was half-way up the ladder, and Abi, as always, was at his shoulder.

Tom climbed out through the hatch after them. He jumped with fright as Amos' voice bellowed out behind him. "Depth?" His deep tones cut clearly through the noise of the battle.

"Mark four," came a voice from the bows.

"You see, Captain, we have very little time." The Master swung round, all but knocking Tom over. "Another fathom and we're done for, sir." Then he glared at Tom. "Get below, boy; you're not wanted in times like these."

"But I'm helping Surgeon Spencer," Tom pleaded, holding his pile of bandages up as proof. The Master grunted, and Tom slipped after his twin to help Francis Medley.

As he knelt on the rough deck and cradled the poor man's sweating face, he could sense the atmosphere around him. Others had heard the Master's words to Captain Grenville, and he was aware of a pause in the flurry of activity. He suddenly realised how much power a captain had.

All eyes were on the "Great Harry". If the *Mary Rose* sank ... Tom tried to imagine what it would be like – the way the water would rush in through the gun ports and fill up the spaces. It would be cold, so cold. He shivered. Then the water would flood over them, rushing into their mouths and noses, and they would die. What would that be like? He'd never even seen the sea before coming on board the *Mary Rose*.

Out of the corner of his eye he saw the Captain and the Master move over to the starboard bow. He held his breath. They were talking in low voices now. He frowned. Why didn't the "Great Harry" turn? But he sort of knew the answer.

"It's fear, isn't it?" Abi's voice was close to his ear, and, as usual, she was sharing his thoughts. "That's why we don't give up. The Captain's afraid of the Admiral, who's afraid of King Henry – and I suppose *he* must be afraid of doing wrong in God's eyes." She peered at the Captain. "Isn't it silly, brother?" she said, her voice unsteady. "I'm not afraid of men's wounds, but I am afraid of the water."

Francis Medley shifted his head in Tom's hands, and immediately, Abi

was back on the job, mopping up the blood that had seeped through the bandaging, and reassuring him that he would be all right. Then the little group began to ease the injured man on to a board, so that they could carry him below.

Moments later, the Master's voice roared out, and the gun crews cheered. Men ran to reset the sails. The deck heaved and trembled, and Tom felt the world turning. The *Mary Rose* was tacking! He crouched to look under the flapping sails, and saw the flagship moving away. For the moment at least, they were safe.

# Abi

The *Mary Rose* rocked gently at anchor in Portsmouth Harbour. The seemingly endless days of wind and rain had gone, leaving the decks to steam and dry in the hot July sunshine. The afternoon watch had nearly come to an end, and the four of them – the twins, Adam and Martin – were leaning against the ship's boat while Henty the lookout boy played a jig on his pipe. A few of the crew were resting, too, but the majority had leave to go on land.

The fighting would start soon. No one doubted that now. Tom said that Amos Wroth couldn't tell when it would start, but there were rumours of a large French fleet waiting to cross the sea to attack them. Abi shivered, despite the heat. Lavenham and Davy and Mary seemed so far away, it was almost as though they had never existed. Thoughts of Pole were never far from her mind, and she sighed. Maybe he would die in the battle. Then there would be no problem.

In the fields around Portsmouth, more and more camps of soldiers were appearing each day, and Southsea Castle was surrounded by the army. There were hundreds of tents in all sorts of colours: red, yellow, green and blue. Three days ago, the townsfolk had held a long procession through the streets. Everyone from the ship had gone to join in, and Abi still remembered the crush of hot, smelly bodies and

the solemn hymn singing. And when they had reached St Thomas' Church, there had been a painful half-hour kneeling on the hard ground while prayers were said, asking God to give King Henry a victory.

She looked up as a shadow fell across her face. Piers stood above her, his hands on his hips.

"Come with me, Kit Penn," he commanded, his haughty tones grating in her ears. "I need to talk to you alone."

Abi stood up reluctantly. What now? She had told him all she knew about Pole. She had nothing to fear from Piers now – especially as he thought she still had the parchment.

She sighed, less in fear than in weariness ... She heard Martin stir, and turned to stop him. "Don't worry," she said. "I'll be all right."

"Come with me," Piers growled, a grumpy look on his face. "I need your help." Abi held back a laugh. Anyone looking less pleased at having to ask for help would be difficult to imagine. She followed him, grinning, as he marched across the deck to an open hatch. His hunched shoulders told her everything.

It was difficult to adjust to the gloom after the brightness of the sunlight. They went along the passageway towards Piers' cabin – but then walked straight past it. Abi's heart thumped in sudden fear. "Piers, where are we going?" she asked in a small voice.

"Where do you think?" He turned back to glance at her, a strange sneer on his face. "I said I need your help. We're going see Captain Grenville."

"But we can't, Piers!" Abi's voice rose to a squeak, but suddenly she was beyond caring about sounding like a girl. This was the end. The Captain was clever. Close up, he would surely realise that she wasn't a boy, even if Piers had never guessed.

"Why not? Don't be ridiculous! I need you to get me out of trouble and

to get Master Pole into trouble. He's found out about my debts, and he's threatening to tell – so I've got to get to the Captain first." Piers paused, realising that Abi was not convinced. "You must," he hissed. "He's killed someone, and don't you forget it."

Abi followed, distraught. Part of her was relieved that at last something was happening, but her stomach turned to water as she imagined the Captain's reaction when he discovered she was a girl.

Piers strode across the last few boards in front of the door to the Captain's cabin, and knocked vigorously. Abi stood limply behind him, her mind icing over. She could run – but where to? There were no fields here. She was trapped. And she was not the only one who would be in trouble – so would Tom and the others, and Surgeon Spencer.

Five minutes later, with the late afternoon sun streaming in through the narrow portholes of the big cabin, Abi found herself standing in front of Captain Grenville. The last thing Piers had said as he pushed her in through the door was to threaten her about what would happen if she mentioned his gambling. "I want to expose my Master so that he won't have a chance of telling the Captain about me. Got it?"

To start with, she didn't know where to look, and she couldn't stop shivering. She knew what fear was – she'd gone cold with fright at the sight of that enormous rat in the hold, only a whisker away from her – but that was nothing compared to this. She longed to be able to curl up in a little ball on the deck and disappear. But instead, she was obliged to stand in the middle of the cabin while Piers explained what he knew.

Then, through the mist of her confusion, she became aware that she was being spoken to. She risked looking up, and saw the Captain's brown eyes watching her intently as he stood there in his breeches and white shirt. He obviously hadn't expected to be disturbed from his

rest. "You are accusing one of my best officers," he said in a low, deep voice that was solemn and vibrant at the same time, reminding Abi of the bass viol she heard in church on Sundays. She couldn't tell whether he was angry or sad.

"Yes – no – I don't know," she stuttered. The last thing she wanted to do was to act as though she was someone who mattered.

"What do you mean?" The great man frowned. "Be careful to tell me the truth."

Abi took a deep breath and started to tell him what Adam had worked out. That Master Pole had been a frequent visitor to the de Vere household. That Master Pole, who had knocked her out of the way all those months ago, had turned out to be the same man she had seen fighting with Master Ferris on deck. The red boots were proof.

"Are you certain?" the Captain snapped. Abi nodded, unable to find the right words.

She crossed her fingers, thinking desperately before each sentence. At one point she had to cough, to stop herself telling him that she'd gone up on deck because she felt sick after scrabbling around to find some boy's clothing. But she kept getting confused, and it all kept coming out in the wrong order. She felt so overwhelmed by the situation she was in. It wasn't usual for an adult to be listening to a child so attentively, and her near-mistake made her feel almost as naked as she was when she threw off her girl's clothes and went to pull on her breeches!

At last she got to the bit where Master Ferris had refused to help Master Pole. "My cousin said he heard them arguing, and he heard Master Ferris threaten Master Pole, saying that he would tell people about the blackmail."

"Blackmail?" The Captain's eyebrows were raised.

Abi crossed her fingers behind her back. This was getting worse. Now

she was betraying Master de Vere. "He was blackmailing the family because they are still of the old faith," she said, in such a low voice that the Captain had to lean across to hear her. "He wanted to marry Mistress Mary de Vere."

The Captain stepped back. He swung round, deep in thought, and paced around the cabin. "And I suppose de Vere said no. Henry always was a bully," he said to himself, almost as though he had forgotten the existence of Abi and Piers. Then, just as abruptly, he turned back to them. "All right, I believe you," he said fiercely, "and I won't tolerate criminals on board. But I can't and won't do anything now. We have a battle to win. So you will not say anything about this, for the moment. Is that understood?"

Piers and Abi nodded.

# Tom

That night, the moon rose high in the sky, spreading a silver path over the marbled sea. Abi had not reappeared. Nor had Piers. One by one, the seamen had clambered back on board as the ships' boats collected them. Another watch change had sounded, food had been eaten – but no one had seen Abi.

An hour after she had gone off with Piers, Tom had climbed down to the orlop deck and shouted into the hold, but there was no sign of her. He checked with Surgeon Spencer – carefully, not wanting to alarm the man – but still no sign. Now he, Martin and Adam were sitting on the deck. He could smell the bittersweet scent of wood smoke drifting across from cooking fires in the town.

"So what are we going to do? She might be anywhere," Martin whispered in a low voice.

"We'd better tell the Surgeon," Adam offered. "At least he might have some ideas."

"Do we tell him she's a girl?" Martin asked. His voice was anxious.

"Do we need to tell?" Tom butted in. "We can't do that – unless we really think she's in danger," he added, seeing Adam's warning face. "We don't want to unless we have to, Adam. Think of all the trouble we'd land in."

"But what if Abi's in trouble because she's already been found out?" Martin said solemnly.

# Abi

It was the day after Piers had forced her to go to the Captain's cabin. For about the tenth time, Abi hauled herself up to the gun deck to fetch medicine from the Surgeon's cabin. Two dozen or more of the ship's crew had sickened with the flux. They lay resting in the ship's hold, where the stench of the ballast was only outdone by the reek of the vomit and diarrhoea running from the men's bodies.

Abi grabbed a white pot, and began measuring out grains of laudanum opiate as the Surgeon had shown her. She mixed the grains with a few drops of oil, then pressed them together and bound each portion into a tiny cloth.

She sighed. Why couldn't she have been born a boy, and why was she unfortunate enough to have seen that monster Pole killing Master Ferris? Slipping the pills into a jar, she climbed down the ladders again, working her way into the depths of the ship, away from the clean, light air above.

It was much more difficult now to walk around the ship. Hundreds of archers had been ferried across, so that there was hardly room to move your feet. She had a nagging stomach ache, although whether that was due to nerves from constantly being on the watch for Pole, she didn't know. The Surgeon was taking no chances, and was constantly dosing her with rose water.

On the orlop deck, she unhooked a lantern and felt her way to the last ladder. She edged forward, her ears registering the constant rumbling of the water against the hull. The patients were slumped around the base of the main mast at the very bottom of the ship, and the old man was still busy tending them.

Without saying much, the Surgeon showed her that he expected the worst. He spent some time examining the men's ears, insisting that Abi should look as well. "A blue spot behind the ear means he will die," he muttered. Abi said nothing. How were they supposed to identify blue spots when the light in the hold was so dim?

At length, the Surgeon stumbled to his feet. "Go up on deck," he said, pushing Abi towards the ladder. "Go and get some air into your lungs while you have time."

"Why while there's time?"

"There'll be more sickness." The old man shook his head knowingly. "The war might be lost before the French ships ever sight our shore if too many sicken." He shooed Abi up the ladder. "You must breathe clean air; I will need your help."

## Tom

Tom was excited, and for a while he blocked out his worries about Pole. The King was giving a banquet for his captains on board the "Great Harry". A banquet before the battle. And the four of them – he, Abi, Adam and Martin – were to be amongst the servers. Best of all, Martin had been asked to play his shawm. Tom had only heard it once, when he had played it for a dance, but he loved the deep, nasal rhythms it produced.

In the end, however, only Martin was sent over to the "Great Harry", and Tom had to be content with watching all the fine nobles being ferried out to the other ship.

After the banquet, the twins stood on deck, watching Martin being ferried back. In the boat with Martin, Piers and the Captain was a black-bearded man, Sir George Carew. It was whispered that he was taking command of the ship, but Tom knew that he wouldn't. Amos had told him as much. "He's only with us for show, young Tom. The Captain's our lord and master still," he'd said. But the boy felt sorry for the Captain. It didn't look right. Not that his face showed anything, but if Tom had been in his position, he would have been very angry. It must be a bit like someone walking into your house and taking over.

The French fleet had appeared. All round them, whistles shrilled as a dozen ships prepared to set off. Across the water came the shouts from Masters and their mates as the crews ran to haul up the dripping anchor cables. On board the *Mary Rose*, Amos Wroth bellowed his orders. Men ran to loosen the sail yards, so that the great mounds of canvas billowed and flapped in noisy confusion. It was difficult, with so many extra foot soldiers crammed on the deck – it was all the crew could do to reach their positions.

"Get some of these men below!" the Master called testily. The archers were herded down the hatches. At last, the sails were brought under control, and one after another, the ships turned into the wind. Beyond the round tower, the vanguard of the French fleet sailed closer, their masts visible across the point.

"They won't get far." Tom turned to find the Master at his shoulder.

"You mean because of the sands?" Tom ventured.

"That's right, lad – the bottom shelves very quickly, and they won't know the whereabouts of the deep water channel. We'll lead them so close they won't be able to turn in time." The Master went back to his work, leaving Tom to keep out of the way. His sister, he realised belatedly, had already moved off. No doubt she was tending to the sick in the hold again.

Following the "Great Harry", the *Mary Rose* tacked through the entrance to the harbour, sailing past the round tower where Tom and Abi had spent the night under an upturned boat all those weeks ago. The town barricade was lined with guns, their bronze muzzles glinting in the sunlight. On they went, past the common land and the yellow-flowered gorse bushes. Ahead lay the dazzling white block of Southsea Castle, where Tom could see the King's court established under the south walls. The King would be able to watch the battle from there.

After the intense heat in the harbour, the cooler air was refreshing. Tom plucked his shirt from his skin and held it loose to let his back dry. He glanced up through the netting which was now stretched over the decks to the brilliant blue sky above. Then he squinted ahead to the approaching French ships with their pennants and flags flying.

He thought of Abi, so far down below the water level that she couldn't possibly know what was happening. Then he stared across at Pole. If the Captain had spoken, the man was hiding his feelings well. Tom shifted uneasily, feeling guilty that he wasn't at his sister's side to guard her, although he knew that she was quite capable of looking after herself. But he didn't move – he couldn't drag himself away from the coming action.

Back on shore, across the common land to the north, he could see a cloud of dust where a column of foot soldiers was still pouring into Portsmouth. The column stretched as far as he could see. Occasionally, the sun touched the points of the hundreds of pikes. It was like looking at a forest of gold.

Tom lifted his head at the first muffled sound of gunfire. He looked

across at Abi. They were both down below, and way above their heads came the thudding reply of their own artillery. Down here, it did not seem so important. Close by the main mast, one man began to gabble incoherently, thrashing out at the air. As carefully as possible, the twins lifted him free of his mates and placed him on his own. He screamed and shuddered, and screamed again. His skin felt cold and clammy.

The ship was tacking; Tom registered the movement and felt a moment's regret at the fact that he was missing the action. The dim, swaying light was mesmerising. They were, he realised in a hellhole all of their own. The shadows and the stench; the constant rumbling of the sea against the wooden sides of the ship; the constant complaining creak as the timbers responded to the motion. It never stopped.

It was a good thing that the *Mary Rose* was so big and strong, he thought. He imagined the ship sinking in battle. They'd never get out, not with those nets strung across the decks. He watched in a dream as Abi stumbled over the ballast with something in her hands. She knelt beside the raving man, and forced a chain of black rosary beads between his fingers. It was odd, he thought, that people still used rosary beads. He couldn't even remember the time when Catholics had been banned from practising their religion, although he knew he had been alive when it happened. But on board ship, no one would worry about a set of beads.

# Abi

The sun had set, and minute by minute the fiery red afterglow faded to dusk and then to darkness. After what seemed like a lifetime down in the hold, Abi breathed the soft, clear air of the cooling day. Part of her watched for Pole, but she was becoming more and more convinced that the Captain had left the confrontation until after the battle. The light breeze stroked her face, and she felt herself nodding with

exhaustion after the long hours below. The three boys sat close by, and she smiled shyly across at Martin.

The English ships had turned south, but as it grew darker, the French had chosen to withdraw. So cowardly, she thought. Now if *she* had been in charge, they wouldn't have turned back! Voices from the town carried across the water to the resting ships. Abi pictured the hundreds of tiny cooking fires beyond the town wall in the army camps. She turned to gaze at the distant bulk of Portsdown Hill, where the warning beacon flared. It was the first in a long line that would stretch right across England. She wondered if Pa and Davy would have a beacon burning near them in Lavenham.

# Tom

"The galleys are coming!" The lookout's high, excited voice cut through the bustle on deck. At once, all the commotion stopped, and everyone turned to stare out over the still water. About two miles away, the blur of oars at work and the long thin shapes of the galleys were visible against the duck-egg blue sky.

Silence.

Then, slowly, a murmur spread along the decks, its echo carrying across from the "Great Harry" to the other vessels anchored nearby. The Master paced up and down the poop deck. "What am I supposed to do?" he grumbled. "How am I supposed to sail into battle when we have a full sea and no wind?" He stopped on the starboard quarter to peer along the length of the *Mary Rose* at the approaching galleys.

"Before we have a quarter ebb, they'll shoot our bows away. There's hardly a piece we can fire on them, they're so low."

Tom sighed. Today would not be easy. He dropped through a hatch to go and help out below. As he waded through the crowded gun deck, voices mumbled uneasily around him. Sounds of explosions followed

him down into the hold, but the ship was not moving. Amos would be tearing his hair out in frustration. Finally, he felt stones under his feet and blinked in the half-dark, trying to adjust to the weird light. He looked around, but Abi wasn't there. His ears caught the sharp, tinny cracks of the lighter swivel guns far above, but the big cannon remained silent.

A hoarse croak from the end of the row of bodies caught Tom's attention. Another man about to become delirious. He groped in his pouch for the rosary beads, and moved towards the sound.

It probably wouldn't make any difference, he thought, but there again, clenching the smooth wooden beads might comfort the man so that he could die more peacefully. The sooner he died, the better for him; the stench down here was unbearable. Tom found he was breathing very lightly to keep the smell of sick bodies out of his nose – but it wasn't very effective!

Where was Abi? Above his head, voices shouted and solid thuds announced that the French gunners were finding their mark. He sighed and stood up. Abi should be here. She shouldn't have wandered off. He started crunching his way across the ballast to climb up and go and find her. Suddenly he staggered, and almost fell. He caught hold of the side of the ladder. It was only when he was half-way up it that he realised what must have happened. The tide had turned!

Higher in the ship, voices called and timbers creaked. Tom pulled himself up to the orlop deck. Yes, Amos was blowing his whistle. He lifted his head and sniffed. The stink and smoke from the gunfire drifted downwards, and through it he could smell the breeze!

# Abi

Abi peered from left to right. From where she was hiding, she could see the steps up to the open deck above her head; she also had a good view each way along the deck. At last it had happened. Just when everybody

was preoccupied with preparing for battle, she'd sensed an enormous male presence towering over her as she knelt by a patient. He didn't have the chance to say anything because Surgeon Spencer had joined her, and then he'd disappeared again, but Abi could feel the man's menacing attitude. He only had to look at her and she was a quivering wreck.

A cheer echoed through the *Mary Rose*. Abi could hear the men on the anchor cable chanting as they helped the ship to break loose. Then there was a tipping sensation, followed by the shrieks of the foot soldiers, who were unused to the sea. More whistles, and the smack of flapping sails. Light flooded the deck as in one great clatter all the gun ports opened and the gun crews sprang to life.

It was so quick that no one noticed – they were all too intent on the battle. A loop of thick rope dropped over Abi's head, and she felt herself being pulled out from behind the steps. She struggled and fought against the powerful grip, one hand holding the rope away from her neck while the other scratched at Pole's arm.

He wrenched her arm down and hissed into her face: "Piers has told me all about you! I found out about his gambling, and we had a terrible argument. Now I'm going to get my revenge on you!" Above them the sails ripped and boomed, and the *Mary Rose* began to turn. The ship heeled, and Pole lost his footing and skidded along the deck, but he clung on to the rope so that the loop tightened round Abi's neck and she could hardly breathe. "De Vere owes me that marriage!" he shrieked as he fell. "All the years I spent looking after that girl!" It was all Abi could do to force her fingers between the noose and her neck. Pole was going mad!

The ship heeled still further. Instinctively, Abi reached out to grab the ladder. The tipping became steeper and steeper. The rope tightened, and she felt herself blacking out as it cut off her breathing. The ship's groaning became a long shriek against the pressure of the sea.

Pole cried out in alarm. He let go of the rope and crashed into the end of a gun carriage, his head banging against the breech end of the gun. His body flopped like a giant rag doll.

Abi wrapped an arm around the bottom step, which was now higher than her head, and pulled herself free of the rope. But then, as the ship continued to slew at an alarming rate, she felt herself flying through the air. She smacked backwards into a seaman's chest. Her back felt as if it had been broken in two.

A gun from the higher side of the deck broke free of its ropes. It hurtled into Pole's lifeless body, and rolled over. Below Abi, someone howled in agony as a gun carriage crunched over his legs.

Everywhere, men were falling and shouting, flailing their arms, trying and failing to stand. Then came an overwhelming roar from below, as the sea flooded into the ship through the open gun ports beneath them. A rush of air blew through the orlop hatch as the dark, churning mass ate its way upwards and along the deck space. The ship shuddered and lost its hold, plunging downwards ...

# Tom

In terror, Tom grabbed at a rope and pulled himself upwards. He didn't know what was happening, but instinct made him crawl on towards the gun deck hatch. The ship shuddered, and he realised that the hold was no longer the bottom of the ship. As the sea swept in, he took a deep breath and struck out towards what he hoped would be a gun port. His hand caught hold of a ring bolt and he clung on to it while water filled the space. In seconds it was clawing up his legs, reaching his waist. He swung on the bolt, kicking at the side of the ship. The water was now nearly over his head. If only he could lever himself through the gun port ... If only he could see Abi ...

# Abi

Taking a last gulp of air as the water washed over her head, Abi let the flood carry her upwards until she was being pressed against the deck. Holding and holding and holding her breath until she thought she would burst, Abi pushed herself out through a gun port and kicked frantically against the ship's outer shell. She moved her arms and legs, keeping her eyes tightly shut. If only she could feel Tom taking her hand . . .

Finally, she stopped struggling. She still hadn't tried to draw breath, and a deep, drowsy feeling came over her . . .

Something hard grazed Abi's head, and in the same instant she broke through the surface of the water. She felt cool air on her face. Her eyes flew open as she choked and coughed. Then she panicked, because this was the first time she'd ever been in the sea. She clutched at the wooden spar that had banged into her. She knew she should look out for the others, but she couldn't find the strength.

Then her hearing cleared, and the thunder of gunfire filled her head: duf, duf, duf, duf. All around her floated the remains of the great *Mary Rose*. Henty's wooden pipe bobbed into view and caught against her spar.

Out of the corner of her eye she saw a figure thrashing about and trying to find a hold. It might be Tom. Just as she was going to shout, a sighing, rushing sound came from the whirlpool which had taken the place of the ship. Then, very slowly, the topmost part of the main mast surged upwards from the water like an enormous monster. Abi shivered, despite the hot sun.

From some way off she heard the systematic plash of oars, but after a

while the sound receded and she knew they had missed her. She felt numb. She found it impossible to accept that the *Mary Rose* had sunk. All she could think of was hanging on to her bit of wood. She couldn't see any one else at all. Somehow she knew she would never see old Surgeon Spencer again, nor Adam – solid, reliable Adam who had given her the comfort she'd never had from her Pa. But she couldn't believe it, and she kept willing his head – or Martin's – to bob up beside her.

A long way off, the guns were still firing. The answering shots were heavy thumps, like doors slamming. Abi kicked herself round to face the land, but realised with a shock that she was being carried along the coast with the flow of the tide.

# Tom

A seagull squealed overhead, and the scent of sun-dried grass sifted through Tom's senses. He opened his eyes and saw a stretch of flat, wet sand. His body felt heavy, and wet, and stiff. Although his brain kept telling his legs to shift, they didn't respond.

"How long has he been there, do you think?" said a familiar voice.

# Abi

"He's alive!" shrieked Abi as Tom's eyes suddenly blinked open.

Martin leaned over and grinned. "So glad you could join us," he said, squeezing Abi's hand. Then, in an effort to act sensibly, he stood up. "We'd better find a campfire and get dry, or we'll catch a chill."

Later, with night folding down around them, the twins slumped in the heat of a campfire in the company of a group of archers. Their fingers

sticky from the great hunks of meat they'd eaten and their minds drowsy with ale, they listened while Martin told their tale. For all they knew, they might be the only survivors.

Abi's eyes misted over at the thought that Adam was truly gone for ever, and tiny Henty, too. She pictured the ship, folded away into the mud for ever. How many people were down there?

One thing she knew for sure was that, somehow, the three of them would stay together. She and Tom ought to let Pa know that they were alive, thought Abi. She realised with a shock that it was half a year or more since she had left Lavenham. And suddenly she longed to go back and see how much tiny Mary had grown, and whether Davy could dress himself yet.

Abi looked at Martin's thoughtful profile against the leaping flames. As he turned to smile down at her, she felt the need to share her thoughts. "We can find another ship, can't we?" she said softly. "I could work on another ship as a surgeon's mate ..."

"Even if you *are* only a girl," Tom said. He grinned as she thumped him playfully over the head.

# Glossary

**Aft**: at the back of the ship

**Ague**: fever

**Almaine**: a Tudor dance

**Amidships**: in the middle section of the ship

**Apothecary**: a chemist

**Aqua menthe**: a warm mint drink given to strengthen the stomach and stop people being sick

**Ballast**: stones in the hold to weigh the ship down and keep it stable

**Bowsprit**: the front mast of the ship, that leans out over the figurehead

**Breeches**: knee-length trousers

**Bulkhead**: a vertical internal wall in the ship, in this case made of wood

**Captain's clerk**: person who was employed to write letters and reports for the Captain

**Captain's Lieutenant of the Militia**: officer in charge of the soldiers on board

**Captain's Steward**: servant to the Captain, in charge of organising food, drink and everything else needed for the Captain's comfort on board

**Companion ladder**: ladder between decks

**Conditte**: open drain, often in the middle of a road, in Tudor times

**Cut-fingered shoes**: shoes, normally fastened with a strap, with slashes in the leather to show the wearer's coloured stockings underneath

**Doublet**: a padded jacket

**Dozen**: twelve

**Fathom**: an old-fashioned way of measuring depth (a fathom:1.83 metres)

**Feet**: a unit of measurement (about 30cm)

**Fighting top**: a lookout platform fixed around the top section of the mast

**Fireboat**: a boat, often an old one, loaded with inflammable material, set alight and sent in the direction of the enemy ships

**Flagship**: the main ship in a fleet

**Flux**: sickness and diarrhoea

**Forecastle**: the front part of the ship, on the top deck

**Forenoon**: the morning

**Forward deck**: deck at the front of the ship

**Galley (1)**: the area in the hold where the crew's meals are prepared

**Galley (2)**: a long low boat rowed by a large gang of men (these were often slaves)

**Gentry chest**: a large wooden box in which wealthy people kept their belongings

**Go about**: to change direction

**Hatch**: a way through to the next deck – normally a square hole with some sort of lifting cover or grid

**Hose**: knitted, coloured tights worn by Tudor men and women

**Larboard**: the left-hand side of the ship

**Last dogwatch**: a watch on duty from 6pm to 8pm

**Linstock**: long carved stick to hold the lighted fuse used to fire the cannon

**Lubbers**: inexperienced sailors

**Lubber's hole**: the hole in the bottom of the lookout's stand, near the top of the mast, that lubbers climbed through rather than going up over the edge of the lookout's stand, which was more dangerous

**Manchet loaf**: a loaf of bread, normally made from white flour

**Mead**: a sweet wine, made with honey

**Navigation**: to direct or plot the course of travel

**Orlop**: the deck above the hold of the ship (below the water level)

**Pike**: a long wooden spear with an iron tip

**Poop**: a high deck built at the back of the ship over the Captain's cabin

**Port (1)**: a harbour that has been organised to cater for big ships

**Port (2)**: the left-hand side of the ship

**Quarter ebb**: the point when the tide is going out and the sea level has dropped by a quarter of its total distance

**Quarterdeck**: the deck behind the main mast (including the poop deck)

**Quartermaster**: a sailor working under the Master of the ship, but in charge of one section of men

**Rope wolding**: rope bound around the mast to keep separate sections held together

**Rosary beads**: prayer beads used by Roman Catholics

**Scribe**: to write

**Scuttle hatch**: a small square-cut hole with grid to allow a way through between decks – a lot smaller than the main hatches

**Shawm**: a musical instrument similar to a clarinet

**Ship's Master**: the man who worked for the Captain and who was responsible for sailing the ship

**Simpling and doubling**: steps in a Tudor dance

**Spars**: cross bars on the mast, holding the sails

**Sprit sail**: a sail attached to the bowsprit, right at the front of the ship

**Starboard tack**: when the ship is sailing with the wind coming across the right side of the ship

**Starboard**: the right side of the ship

**Steward**: a senior servant

**Surgeon's mate**: boy or young man working for the Surgeon

**The hold**: the bottom section of the ship

**Touch hole**: the hole on the top of a ship's gun where the fuse is lit

**Tumblehome**: the side-walls on the weather deck, bending slightly inwards, which had to be climbed over to get on board

**Vanguard**: the first section of the fighting force

**Weather deck**: the open deck – open to the weather

**Weevil**: a beetle

**Yards (sail yards)**: long lengths of wood strung from the masts that held the square sails

**Yeomen**: farmers

**Younkers**: ordinary sailors